ROUSTABOUT

CARNIVAL OF MYSTERIES

MORGAN BRICE

CONTENTS

eBook ISBN: 978-1-64795-052-1
Print ISBN: 978-1-64795-053-8

Roustabout, Copyright © 2023 by Gail Z. Martin.
Cover by Dianne Thies
The Carnival of Mysteries, Errante Ame, Madame Persephone, and Peter the Potion Master © 2023 Ari McKay, used with permission.

Darkwind Press is an imprint of DreamSpinner Communications, LLC

To everyone who believes in the magic of love

CHAPTER ONE

RJ

*R*J Tucker sat at the bar at Haggerty's in Memphis and nursed a Jack and Coke. He had a feeling he could get lucky tonight; wasn't sure he wanted to.

Whiskey wouldn't calm his nerves, at least not what he dared consume this close to a job. A good, hard fuck usually took the edge off, which is why he lingered over his drink, wondering who might wander in.

He'd given up on Mr. Right, but he was just fine with Mr. Right-now.

His jobs required staying in shape, filling out his six-foot tall frame with muscle. And coupled with his shaggy red hair, scruffy beard, and green eyes, RJ didn't go begging for bed partners when he was in the mood.

"Bourbon, neat. Double." The tall man slid onto the barstool next to RJ, bumping shoulder and hip in a way that RJ knew wasn't accidental. He counted to ten before he turned to look, already approving of the man's voice, deep like the rumble of a V8 engine, and his choice of liquor.

RJ's gaze flicked over the newcomer. He was probably a good four inches taller, just the kind of rangy build RJ liked. The cut of the man's short chocolate-brown hair suggested military or law enforcement, either past or present. That upped the risk of a liaison, but RJ usually appreciated the rush of danger.

"Been rainin' all day. Think it might never stop," the stranger said, and since there was no one on his other side and the bartender had gone to fetch his order, the comment was clearly directed at RJ.

"Don't mind getting wet, now and again. Does a fellow good." If the guy was looking to get laid, he'd pick up on the insinuation. If not, RJ probably wouldn't have to fight his way out of a brawl over it.

"Is that so?" The man chuckled, a low, throaty sound that went right to RJ's groin. He felt himself chub, despite his earlier ambivalence.

"Seems like the night for it." RJ had been doing this dance since he was eighteen with a fake ID, navigating the iffy politics of southern bars where taking a glance or a comment the wrong way was the difference between getting laid and getting laid out.

At twenty-eight, RJ had crossed a lot of things off his bucket list, but finding a partner for more than a roll in the sheets wasn't one of them, and he doubted it ever would be. *Maybe when I finish the job—if I live to tell the tale. Probably not. Don't really want to lie, and I can't tell the truth.*

The tall man's knee bumped his, another non-accident. RJ noticed how large the stranger's hand was as it wrapped around the whiskey glass and pictured those fingers curling around his cock. *Wonder if his dick's proportional? He'd be a hell of a ride if it is.*

They nursed their drinks, acutely aware of each other, trading light comments and furtive glances full of intention.

After they finished, Tall Guy slid a couple of bills over the bar and stood, stretching to give RJ a good view of his fine ass and the curve of his back.

"Gonna hit the head," he said quietly, like the invitation they both knew it was.

RJ nodded and paid his own tab in cash before the man walked away, a signal that he'd follow.

Moments later, after a delay that didn't fool anyone, RJ walked into the restroom. The place smelled like piss, sex, and cheap cologne, with a larger-than-average vending machine full of condoms and lube and stalls big enough for two.

Tall Guy looked up from where he washed his hands in the sink and gave RJ a sexy smirk. RJ raised an eyebrow, daring the other man to make the first move.

Those long fingers closed around RJ's wrist, pulling him into a stall, and the muscular, lanky body pressed him up against the wall.

"No marks," Tall Guy rumbled from where his face was buried in RJ's neck. "And no kissing on the lips."

Tall Guy pushed his thigh between RJ's legs, giving them both friction. From the hard length pressed against his groin, RJ decided that the man was *definitely* proportional.

RJ ran a hand over his partner's very firm chest, stroking his nipples through his shirt until they hardened to nubs. Tall Guy mouthed at RJ's temple, chin, and throat, never quite sucking or biting, not exactly a kiss. His hair had a sandal-wood and vanilla smell and beneath that a heady mix of sweat and fresh grass.

Big hands moved over RJ's body, down his biceps, across his chest, and around to give his ass a squeeze. For a second, RJ thought the man meant to pick him up, have RJ wrap his legs around his waist, and fuck him against the wall. Another time, that would get RJ's motor revving, but not tonight.

"Hand job," RJ blurted. That beat coming in his pants if they kept rubbing off on each other, and he didn't want to ruin his best jeans by going to his knees on the dirty bathroom floor.

"Works for me." Tall Guy's throat was so close to RJ's cheek that he could feel the vibration of his vocal cords and a delicious rasp of stubble.

Normally RJ would have flipped their positions so he wasn't caged in by the big man's long arms. He always left himself a way to make a quick escape. Something about this guy didn't set off RJ's alarms, and maybe that alone should have made him question, but he was too hard to care.

RJ fixed the stranger's good looks in his mind for nights when he was alone with his own hand. Blue eyes, high cheekbones, perfect nose. *Why is a guy who looks like him humping a stranger in a tavern bathroom?*

He quit thinking when a large hand worked his belt open, then eased the zipper down. The man spit into his calloused palm and wrapped his fingers around both their rock-hard cocks. Pre-come eased the slide, which was still a little on the rough side like RJ preferred. It had been too long, and he knew he wouldn't set a record for stamina.

Good thing I'm never going to see him again so there's no need to be embarrassed.

He wasn't sure which of them came first, but it was close, mere seconds apart, their grunts leaving nothing to the imagination of anyone who might wander into the room. Hot jizz fountained over the stranger's hand, and he kept pumping until they were both spent.

Tall Guy wiped his hand on a wad of toilet paper and flushed the evidence before tucking himself back in and zipping up. RJ did the same. From the noises in the other stalls, the bathroom's only other occupants were too distracted to notice when the two of them walked out and went to the sink.

"Thanks for the ride." Tall Guy gave a nod like the tip of a hat and headed for the door.

Well, that's clear. No going back to a room, no second round. Didn't ask for my name, didn't give his. Adios, amigo.

RJ couldn't help being curious and waited a moment after the man left to look out at the parking lot. He'd figured the guy had a nice pickup but didn't expect the sleek black Corvette Stingray that pulled away.

"Damn." Now RJ's imagination was going to work overtime to make sense of the contradictions. High-and-tight haircut cruising a gay bar. Clearly not wanting entanglements. Country enough to fit in at a place like Haggerty's, but city enough to drive a 'Vette.

Hot as hell, fucks like a porn star, and he's mysterious too? Shit. I might be in love.

He'd settled his tab, so RJ walked back to his second-hand Chevy Impala, the vehicle that suited his latest job. Tomorrow he'd go to work, but tonight he had time to review his plans, settle into the persona the job required, and try not to overthink what had to be done.

RJ paid cash for the room at a motel on the outskirts of town. The place was a little too hard-used to qualify as vintage or retro, but the mattress wasn't buggy, and the AC worked, so RJ didn't complain.

Now that he'd worked off some jitters, it was time to prepare. RJ took his dopp kit into the bathroom and spread a large piece of plastic over the sink. He took out a pair of barber's shears and trimmed his shaggy hair, not as short as Tall Guy's, but perfect for Middle America conservative. The beard was next to go, and RJ sighed as he shaved it off, promising himself he would grow it back when this was all over.

The plastic caught all the hair. RJ wrapped it up neatly and shoved it into a trash bag, then put it in his suitcase. Tomorrow, he'd sweep up any remainders and wipe down any surfaces he'd touched to obliterate his prints. It was habit not to touch more than was absolutely necessary.

RJ applied the brown hair dye with practiced strokes, making sure to get his eyebrows as well. Tomorrow, a pair of colored contacts would change his green eyes to brown, completing the transformation.

He hung up the suit he'd gotten at a thrift store in Nashville. RJ needed to look professional but not slick and sell his expertise without being intimidating. The fabric and the cut were clearly discount store, as were the shoes. To sell the con, he needed to be what Joss Carmody envisioned as a "Christian Investment Advisor," based on what he'd seen on television since RJ knew the man had never been inside a bank in his life.

Only one more job after this one, and then I'm off to Key West or maybe the Maldives, he promised himself. That wasn't the absolute truth, but it wasn't exactly a lie, either. The dream of relaxing on a white sand beach and leaving all this behind him soothed RJ's soul on dark nights, a pleasant fantasy. The odds of surviving and eluding his past and his would-be jailers weren't in his favor.

He took a deep breath and blew it out, shaking his arms to loosen his shoulders and intentionally unclenching his jaw.

"You've got this." He eyed his reflection in the mirror. "You know the Carmodys better than anyone else on your list. Joss is going to eat this up, and by the time it goes south, he'll never know what hit him."

All his jobs required research and planning, but this one in particular had taken plenty of preparation. RJ had set up the fake social media accounts and gradually befriended people in Carmody's circle, commenting on their posts, offering investment advice for free, being helpful. Sock puppet accounts added glowing reviews. When those tips—gleaned from reading the financial magazines foreign to Carmody's crowd—paid off, RJ accepted their accolades with aw-shucks modesty and asked for referrals, which led right where he wanted—Joss Carmody.

He knew how to hide his IP address, conceal his digital footprint, posting through a VPN, from libraries or on motel and coffee shop Wi-Fi, using pawn shop-purchased unregistered laptops. The cell phone in his pocket was a pay-by-the-minute burner, untraceable.

RJ had paid cash for the Impala, bought from a security guard at a senior citizens' apartment building. The owner recently died and had no family to come for his belongings—including the car. That meant the plates were legit, and the car hadn't been reported stolen. If and when anyone noticed, RJ planned to be long gone.

Or at least, "Isaac Jamison" would be history. Another change of hair color, different contacts, trimmed stubble instead of a beard, new clothes, and RJ would become someone else, abandoning the social media sites and setting up for the next job before he could finally close the book on the first half of his life.

He stared at himself in the mirror once more, searching in vain for any trace of the frightened young boy he had been when he'd run away from his abusive foster parents. *It's been thirteen years. Will they recognize me?*

His voice was deeper, a man's tone instead of a squeaky adolescent's, and his body had filled out once he discovered the difference sufficient food and sleep made. No longer a scrawny, cowering kid, not "sickly" anymore after he'd learned that normal people went to doctors instead of relying on cheap folk cures that didn't work.

7

Hidden in a locker at the Nashville Greyhound station was every sordid detail he'd compiled on the Carmodys. After tomorrow, when the fix was in, RJ planned to turn the evidence over to a reporter hungry for a new social ill to avenge who didn't mind anonymous sources.

If the job went right, no one else would suffer what RJ and his siblings had endured, at least not from the Carmodys.

RJ knew his spiel, but he forced himself to run through the presentation on his laptop one more time. He'd rehearsed until he knew the words by heart, then practiced some more until he could sound conversational. RJ had even tweaked his accent, the better to go unrecognized, with just enough of a drawl to earn trust as a fellow Southerner but more citified than the Appalachian twang he'd been raised with.

He looked longingly at the whiskey bottle on the dresser and resisted its pull. Joss Carmody was a hard drinking man, but even he might not be fool enough to take money advice from a guy who smelled like the bottom of a cask.

Instead, RJ stripped off his clothes and turned the shower on hot, hoping it would loosen tense muscles. He kept his newly dyed hair out of the spray, but let the water play over his shoulders and chest, then lower to wash away the dried come from his encounter at the bar.

Here in the shower, he could jerk off without the risk of leaving behind DNA in the sheets. RJ slicked his hand and worked his cock just the way he liked it, rolling and tugging his balls, stroking over the sensitive head.

He remembered the strength in Tall Guy's long fingers and big hands, the scrape of calluses and short, well-kept nails. RJ recalled the way the stranger smelled, the rumble of his voice, the heft of the body that pinned him against the wall, and the muscles in the arms that caged him in, a willing prisoner.

This time, RJ meant to take his time, drag it out, unlike the hurried encounter at the bar, but his body had other plans. He came faster than he wanted, and his orgasm hit like a freight train, surprising for a second round, leaving him weak in the knees.

"Damn," he murmured when he could think again. *It hasn't been like that with anyone since...well, never that I can recall. Too bad I won't see him again. He'd make a mighty fine friend with benefits.*

RJ cleaned up, soaping away the evidence and watching it swirl down the drain. The cheap towels scratched as he dried off. Another glance in the mirror assured him that his dye job hadn't run. He brushed his teeth and swirled mouthwash to kill any lingering scent of whiskey, then pulled on his boxer briefs and a T-shirt and crawled beneath the rough sheets.

One more job after this, and I can leave fucking god-forsaken Tennessee behind forever.

He fell asleep dreaming of a beach in the Maldives, making out in a cabana with Tall Guy, and sipping drinks within sight of the ocean, leaving his name, his history, and his record dead and buried.

The next day, promptly at ten in the morning, RJ pulled up in front of an old house at the end of an unpaved driveway. The aged two-story might have been comfortable long ago, but it clearly hadn't been well cared for in many years. *They don't take care of anything—or anyone. Guess that hasn't changed.*

White paint peeled from the weathered clapboards, a few shutters were missing and others hung askew. The roof bowed, and the remaining shingles were long past their prime. RJ couldn't help wondering which kid had to sleep in the leaky room and whether the rats made it up to the attic.

A rattletrap minivan sat under a tree next to the house.

Behind it was a garage that RJ suspected held the pricy bass boat, a new pickup, and expensive hunting gear Carmody had bought recently. He counted six kids in the yard ranging from a toddler to a skinny boy who looked about twelve. The older kids sat under a thick oak, talking or napping, while the younger ones played with rocks and sticks.

A boy ran forward, clearly having been dared, as the younger kids tittered.

"Who are you, mister? You from the County? Better leave. Mr. Joss don't like the County folks."

RJ thought he had steeled himself for this, but he couldn't help the way his breath hitched. The boy's shirt was stained and faded, and his torn jeans were a half-inch too short to be fashionable. The others didn't look any better dressed, with lank hair and the kind of shadow left on skin by old dirt when baths were too far between. He looked for bruises but knew from experience that Carmody was too smart to hit where it showed.

The worst thing was, RJ suspected the kids were wearing their best clothing because "company" was coming. Sense memory slammed into him, the itch of unwashed skin, the unmistakable smell of body odor and dirty hair, the shame of looking poor. A flash of rage followed because all that had been unnecessary, the result of adults who'd been trusted with money and responsibility and failed miserably to do the right thing.

"No, I'm not with the County." RJ knew that the boy meant Child Protective Services. He'd seen Joss Carmody run more than one agent off with a shotgun back in the day after sending his charges into the woods and threatening them if they spoke their truth.

Easy. Don't blow it. I'm going to fix this and make sure the Carmodys can't do this to anyone ever again. Work the plan. Throw up later.

"Justin—don't bother that man. All of you, quit lollygagging and get to your chores."

Thirteen years hadn't changed the burly, red-faced man on the porch as much as RJ had expected. Gray shaded Joss Carmody's long hair, slicked back in an attempt to impress his guest. He wore a clean, collared shirt—probably the one he saved for the rare occasions when a public appearance was necessary. The beer gut was a little bigger, and when RJ looked close, he swore the man's alcoholism had begun to show in his face.

"You must be Mr. Jamison." Carmody's attempt at friendliness came off skeevy and obsequious. He held out a beefy hand, and RJ forced himself to shake it, squelching a flinch at the memories of all the times that hand had wielded a belt.

"I'm real thankful you came out here to see us." Carmody ignored the kids who had scattered, but not vanished. "I've heard good things about you. I think you might be the answer to our prayers."

RJ had a flash of the irony of a con man conning a con man. Carmody knew exactly what phrases would ease suspicion and signal the minimum propriety to keep authorities at bay. That included an easy-going demeanor to negate suspicion of rough treatment and enough references to Jesus to signal upright morals.

RJ knew Carmody's vices and weakness, and he'd had more than a decade to figure out how to play him like a fiddle.

To RJ's relief, Carmody didn't look too closely at him, and didn't give any sign of recognition. Then again, RJ was playing a part, so Carmody didn't have to see a person, just a role that would get him what he wanted. Which was always more money.

Thankfully, this wasn't any of the houses RJ had lived in under the Carmodys' care. It fit the mold—big, rundown, and cheap. They wouldn't stay more than a few years before they'd move again, counting on an overburdened, under-staffed and apathetic social services system to turn a blind eye.

The inside of the house looked just as hard-used, with the fresh smell of bleach telling RJ that a quick tidying up had put the place respectable enough to avoid censure.

"This here's the missus." Carmody nodded toward the woman sitting at the kitchen table who didn't bother to rise and barely acknowledged RJ's presence.

Molly Carmody had never mothered the foster kids in her care, even as she went through the minimum efforts required to keep them fed and clothed. Cigarettes had pinched lines around her pale lips and yellowed her teeth, but the mean set to her mouth hadn't changed. She would put up with Joss's assholery until she snapped, taking out her bottled rage on whoever was closest or too slow.

Work the plan, and they'll get what's coming to them—and the kids will get out.

"Can I get you some coffee, Mr. Jamison? Molly—go make a fresh pot," Joss ordered.

"No, really, please don't bother. I want to focus on what I came to share with you. Let's get started, shall we?" RJ set up his laptop, and out of the corner of his eye saw Joss sizing him up—his suit, his watch, the brand of computer. When Joss licked his lips and sat back in his chair, RJ knew he'd baited the trap correctly.

"I see you have a large family," RJ said as the laptop booted.

"They're not family," Molly snapped. "Just the current crop of kids."

RJ froze for a second before learned trauma responses and long experience gave him the ability to keep moving. The Carmodys had always considered their fosters as a "crop" to be harvested—bringing in their stipend until they aged out of the system or ran away.

"Molly's a kidder, she's always joking around." Joss's eyes narrowed when he looked at his wife, whose blank stare pretended he didn't exist.

"I'm sure that money's tight. Everyone can always use more, right?" RJ had hacked their bank account, so he knew exactly how much their current batch of children brought in and how little of it went back out to pay for food, clothing, medical care, or other necessities.

On the other hand, a new bass boat, expensive fishing equipment, pricy hunting gear, and liquor clearly held priority when it came to paying bills. Not to mention Joss's gambling addiction, which apparently hadn't improved over time.

"That's the truth. God knows, everything gets more expensive all the time—especially for the kids." Joss sat next to Molly, who didn't seem to register his presence.

"That's why the Lord has laid it on my heart to share this with you." RJ let himself sink into being Isaac Jamison so he could forget what RJ Tucker didn't want to remember. "I realize that we know a lot of the same people, but I haven't shown them what I'm going to show you. You're serving a higher purpose, and I want to help you get the results you deserve."

Carmody licked his lips again. "What do you have in mind? I don't trust the stock market."

RJ shook his head. "No stocks. Am I right that the stipends you get for the children are tax free and don't count as income?" He knew they didn't, but he needed to get Carmody agreeing to build buy-in.

"That's right. We put it in the bank for a rainy day."

That was bullshit, but RJ kept his expression pleasant. "What would you say if I could show you a way to double or triple your investment every few months—and do it in a way that the government wouldn't know, so they won't come after the gains?"

Greed glinted in Carmody's eyes. "You can do that? How?"

"Cryptocurrency." RJ dropped his voice to share the secret, even though it was just the three of them. "Completely legal to buy, but then the banking is done offshore where there aren't reporting requirements. Untraceable. You can get to it but the feds can't. Does that sound like something you'd be interested in?"

By the time RJ took them through the couple of slides on the computer showing charts with spiking gains and glowing praise from newly rich "investors," Joss was ready to sign and even Molly had stirred from her torpor.

"How do we get started?" Joss asked, and RJ could practically see dollar signs dancing in the man's eyes.

"I can purchase the crypto for you as soon as I have cash. But there's a minimum. You need at least fifteen thousand to buy in."

Joss stilled. "That's a lot of money."

RJ raised his hands palm up in a gesture of resignation. "I'm sorry. I don't make the rules." He moved to close his laptop.

"Wait. I can get it for you. How do you need it?"

He knew Joss had at least double that much in the bank, a sum that shouldn't have been possible if he and Molly had been spending the stipends on the children.

RJ also knew from his foray into their account and his sleuthing that Joss's under-the-table job as a night desk clerk at a crummy motel and his fraudulently obtained disability benefits didn't cover his expensive purchases, let alone pay household expenses. Losing the ability to have fosters would protect the kids and punish the Carmodys in the way that would hurt the most—their pocketbook.

"We want to keep this from tripping government notice," RJ reminded him. "Don't want them sniffing around. That means splitting this into two transactions. You'll get a receipt, of course. And notification when the crypto hits the account I'll set up for you offshore. Then you sit back and watch that untaxed money roll in. When you want some, just use the debit card we'll send you."

There was no crypto, no account, no card. But by the time Joss wised up, RJ would be in the wind, the crusading investigative reporter would have the dossier turned into a hot exposé, and a dozen sock puppet accounts would blast out incriminating details to shame authorities into removing the children and sending them to hopefully better homes.

The checks, voided but evidence of intended fraud, would seal the case.

Joss licked his lips again, but the greed in his eyes hadn't lessened. If Molly had reservations, she had learned a long time ago to keep her mouth shut.

"You want cash? Always like to keep some on hand for emergencies," Joss said, although RJ knew it was for gambling. Running him short had the added benefit that the people he owed would react badly if his debts weren't paid.

"The company needs a check, made out to Cryptocurrency Investments," RJ told him. "One check for nine thousand, dated today, and the other for six more, dated four days from now. They're both under the federal reporting limit. The market is always moving, so the sooner I can buy in for you, the quicker you start seeing your investment grow. My take is three percent."

RJ didn't intend to pocket any cash at all, and the transaction wouldn't actually be completed, but he knew Joss would believe the hoax more quickly if he understood what was in it for "Isaac."

Joss left the room and came back with his checkbook. Molly barely blinked. RJ figured he'd had his first lessons in disassociation from her, an uncomfortable revelation. He watched Joss like he was observing from outside his body, Jamison and not RJ, not little Ricky Jon.

"Good enough?" Joss said, and RJ tucked the two checks into his bag along with his computer.

"I'd better get to the bank so I can get this set up for you before the end of the banking day." RJ knew that keeping up the urgency would focus Joss so he didn't start having second thoughts. His skin crawled just being near the man.

"Remember—if anyone asks, you don't have to explain why you need your own money." RJ rose to leave. "It's none of their damn business."

The twist to Joss's lip made it clear that RJ's comment played to his anti-authority streak. "You got that right."

This was the vulnerable moment, when a smarter mark might turn on RJ and call the cops. Joss wasn't that man, and his greed far outpaced any internal caution. That didn't stop RJ from sweating bullets as he promised to be in touch and headed for his car.

The kids weren't in sight, but RJ knew they were probably watching from somewhere. Molly likely hadn't moved except to light a smoke or pour a drink.

"It takes a couple of days to process, but you'll definitely hear by Friday," RJ told Joss, who had followed him out. Three days was plenty of time for the reporter to write his "scoop" and the social media accusations to go viral.

"Thanks, man. You're an answer to prayer." Joss thumped a hand on the car roof.

RJ forced himself to smile and make it look real. *I'm definitely answering Ricky Jon's prayer to make the bad people go away. Sometimes if the gods don't answer, you've got to do things yourself.*

Once he was miles away from the house, RJ pulled into a parking lot. He called the reporter from a burner phone, leveraging another relationship he'd carefully nurtured for when the time was right. The man jumped at the story of a former youth pastor gone foster child fraudster, and RJ promised to call him back with the combination to the bus station locker with the dossier after he'd had a chance to add the voided but incriminating checks.

Everything in the folder had been printed on library or office center printers, so there was no "printer signature" for anyone to follow. RJ emphasized the imminent danger to the kids in the Carmodys' care, and the reporter promised a breaking news exclusive by the morning's news cycle.

He'd already programmed the social media posts through accounts he'd set up for that purpose, ones that couldn't be traced back to him. They would begin the chant for accountability that, together with the news story, would bring down the Carmodys and save the kids.

RJ drove to Nashville to slip the checks into the dossier at the bus station, then headed back to Memphis, where he could hide in the bustle of the city.

Before he had gone to see the Carmodys, he had replaced the "clean" license plate on his car with another he'd bought off a guy at a dicey salvage yard. He stopped behind an abandoned shopping plaza and switched the plates back, then ditched the salvage plate in a dumpster. If any cameras had seen him driving to or from the house, there would be no plate to find. The sedan itself was common and unremarkable, hard to identify.

Once he had gone a comfortable distance, RJ went to a string of grocery stores and drug stores where he bought reloadable gift cards, each for a few hundred dollars, which he paid for in cash. Then he stopped at the library for a computer and used the cards to make three transactions.

One went to a shelter for runaways and homeless former foster kids. Another donation went to a shelter for battered women with substance abuse issues. He closed his eyes and thought of his mother as he pressed send. The third went to a carefully vetted organization that fought against dangerous conditions for warehouse workers. Sending the donations had become part of his ritual each time he finished a job.

RJ found a motel and washed out the temporary hair dye, mussing his hair to look less like the type of guy who might go house to house asking if people knew Jesus. He lingered in the shower, jerking off to thoughts of the guy from Haggerty's, remembering the press of his tall body, the feel of the stranger's calloused palm on his dick, how he knew to squeeze and stroke just right. He came hard and fast, a combination of frustration and the need to let off steam from the day's stress.

The lukewarm water poured over RJ's body as he trembled through the aftershocks, wishing he wasn't alone, that his imaginary lover was solid and real—and in his bed. With a sigh he shut off the water and toweled off, reminding himself what a terrible idea it would be to go back to Haggerty's looking for a second round.

Don't backtrack. No entanglements. I don't want to spend the rest of my life in jail.

RJ took out the contact lenses and changed into a sweatshirt and jeans, then stopped at the store and picked up a handle of bourbon for later.

To celebrate, he bought himself the biggest steak the local steakhouse had to offer, a Porterhouse that came with a loaded sweet potato, blue cheese salad, hot rolls with honey butter, and a slab of chocolate cake for dessert.

RJ didn't feel guilty, but the elation he had imagined

didn't materialize, even when he poured himself a few fingers' worth of bourbon back in his room and raised a toast.

Getting the kids out of the Carmodys' care wouldn't happen immediately, much as RJ wished he could have grabbed them all and drove away. He was trusting a broken system to do its job, something his badly shaken faith resisted from past disappointments.

If the system worked, I wouldn't be doing this.

That's where the reporter's exposé and the social media agitation came in, forcing authorities to do their jobs through public humiliation. It might stop the Carmodys, but RJ knew there were other bad foster situations out there that would go on, other kids lost in the bureaucracy.

I can't save them all. But I can take one bad player off the board. Hey, Ricky Jon, he said to the memory of his younger self. *Another one down. One more to go. I'm keeping my promise.*

CHAPTER TWO

Bart

"You're going to be chasing a ghost," Assistant Director Boward told him.

"Good thing I'm a necromancer." Bartlett Gibson grinned, but his smile quickly faded. "What really happened to the guy I'm replacing?"

Boward waved him toward a chair and Bart sat in front of the man's desk. The director slid a fat dossier toward him. "I know you read the brief online, but the folder has the details. Hank Whetherby was a good agent, twenty years in the Bureau. Damn good psychic too. The life caught up with him. Bad ticker. Widow-maker heart attack. Dead before he hit the ground."

"That's too bad," Bart replied, although the answer didn't surprise him. Lots of guys in this business went out like that, if it wasn't from a bullet or a knife.

"Lucky for us, Hank took good notes," Boward added.

"Understood. I'll dive in right away. Is there other media? Closed-circuit clips, photos, audio, social media trail?" Bart couldn't remember ever having a case that didn't come with digital downloads.

Boward shook his head. "No. That's why we call the perp Ghost Boy. We don't have a name, a scrap of DNA evidence, or even a fingerprint. Zilch. Whoever he is, he's very good at what he's doing. Which is why we want to nail him before he moves on to bigger fish."

"You think he's been practicing?" The overview had been clear on the charges—identity theft, impersonating credentialed authorities, possible money laundering, and a slew of related allegations that would put Ghost Boy away for a long time. What was missing was any arrest record, background on the lead suspect, or motive.

"That was Hank's best guess," Boward replied. "The attacks have been random. Hank thought it suggested that Ghost Boy was stress-testing different systems, looking for weaknesses, ramping up for bigger targets. We figure that's also why he's avoiding hits in major cities. Rural areas have fewer protections, looser systems."

"Hmm." Bart withheld judgment. "Interesting. And I'm sure it's in the file—which I'll read thoroughly—but none of the marks knew why they'd been targeted?"

"*Why* they were hit really isn't hard to figure out. They're all crooked. Narrowing it down to *who* is the hard part."

Bart knew better than to say what he was thinking out loud. *If that's the case, he's doing our job for us. Why are we chasing him so hard?*

He accepted that he had an unorthodox perspective on that subject, one better left unexamined by the higher-ups.

"Have you gotten settled?" Boward switched subjects.

Temporarily relocating from Nashville to Memphis went with the assignment. In eight years with the Tennessee Bureau of Supernatural Investigation, Bart had done stints all over the state for anywhere from a few weeks to months at a time. Memphis was far better than some of the small towns which had felt like exile.

Bart hadn't made a secret of being gay when he applied to the TBSI, and his current supervisors had been supportive. But having grown up in the state, Bart had no illusions about how many other residents—and politicians—felt about it. That meant remaining guarded, watching his back, and flying under the radar.

"I found a place that'll be fine." The Bureau had given him a list of short-term and extended-stay rentals that were cleared for security and reimbursement. Bart had found a comfortable one-bedroom apartment within walking distance of food and necessities. Most importantly, it had good Wi-Fi. "I moved in over the weekend and had a look around."

"Good. I don't know that you'll get much of a chance to sightsee, but Memphis is an awesome town for terrific food and great music. Might as well make the most of it while you're here."

"Thank you, sir." Bart reached out for the thick file, knowing what his evening held.

"Good luck," Boward replied. "Ghost Boy's hard to predict without a pattern, but if anyone can figure it out, I think you will. Maybe you can get the spooks to help you."

Bart gave a strained smile. "I'll see who I can rustle up."

His abilities as a witch and a necromancer were prized by the Bureau in equal measure. However, those talents made some people uncomfortable around him in a way that had nothing to do with his being gay. His magic and his affinity for summoning spirits were proven and documented. They also creeped his peers out, guaranteeing that he worked alone.

For the most part, that suited Bart fine. While the TBSI sought agents with abilities, necromancy remained rare, and people's opinions were too often forged by fantasy novels and video games. He'd had partners who treated his gift like a parlor trick, and others who were so desperate to reconcile with their own ghosts that they regarded Bart with awe instead of working together as equals. He'd gotten used to being on his own.

"Keep me posted on your progress. Stop by the office if you need something—call ahead and we'll have it ready for you," Boward told him. "Log your time. You know the drill."

Bart thanked him, slipped the folder into his messenger bag, and headed out. The few agents who were working in the bullpen turned as he walked by, curious about their new temporary coworker. Bart nodded and kept going. Nobody hailed him, and he didn't stop to make conversation. He was in Memphis on special assignment, and they all knew he'd be gone soon.

He hadn't quite figured out the neighborhood restaurants yet, so he ordered both his groceries and his dinner online. A cooler full of perishables from his Nashville apartment and a couple of bags of staples would tide him over for a few days, until he could find a new grocery store and try out the restaurants that delivered.

Bart had given himself a rare indulgence of going out on the town for a few hours the previous night to celebrate endings and beginnings. Tomorrow, more exploring might be fun. Today, he wanted to unpack, get comfortable, and dig into the file. Something about this case tugged at his intuition, telling him there might be more than his predecessor assumed. The scant details intrigued Bart and promised a more interesting pursuit than the usual fake psychics and fraudulent witches.

Bart had moved his suitcase and other bags from his car into the living room, put a few items into the refrigerator, and changed from a T-shirt and jeans into a suit and tie for his stop at the office. Now, he changed into sweats, relieved at loosening his tie and unbuttoning his shirt.

Everything he had brought in sat exactly where he left it, which was both a relief and sad in a way Bart didn't want to examine.

He pushed away the melancholy and got busy stuffing clothing into the tall dresser, hanging his suit in the closet, and hooking up his gaming system. Bart carried a few things into the kitchen—the makings for emergency pasta, some favorite snacks, and a fifth of his favorite bourbon.

The apartment had a living room with a couch and table, a galley kitchen, full bathroom, and a bedroom with a king bed, dresser, and chest of drawers. That gave him room to stretch his long legs and a door to separate his work from his private quarters. Bart had made do with worse. The furniture—all in shades of dark blue and gray—looked relatively new, the apartment and appliances were clean, and the building's security was adequate.

Just to be safe, he'd already checked out the fire stairs, assured himself that the alarms worked properly, and walked the area nearby enough to have several escape routes in mind, if necessary. His Corvette had a reserved parking spot nearby in the building's garage.

Bart placed a grocery order and found a Chinese restaurant that delivered. While he waited, he double-checked the rooms for any ghostly or witchy supernatural presence, chalked protective sigils and runes, salted the windows, vents, and outside doors, and said a cleansing spell.

Then he made a pot of coffee and settled in on the couch with the file.

As with the overview document he'd seen, the dossier had no information at all on the suspect, which alone was highly unusual. Bart wondered how the string of crimes could be attributed to a single perpetrator when there was no person of interest.

A quick glance told him that the lack of any incriminating evidence and the relative similarity of the incidents had been enough to get the crimes grouped together. That was odd, but at worst it might mean later treating them as one-offs with different suspects. If the hunch that led to bundling the situations panned out, he could close several cases at once.

Agent Whetherby had been thorough, Bart allowed as he started in on the notes. It took a few pages before he caught onto Whetherby's jagged handwriting.

The first case involved a well-off businessman—Dennis Abbot—in Jackson, owner of a metalworking company. Abbot claimed that a man named Andrew Benchley convinced him to invest in a logistics company that would cut costs, speed deliveries, and dramatically improve his profits, persuading him that his only hope of surviving a competitive market was to make a very large investment. Unfortunately, Abbot embezzled company money to authorize the deposit. Benchley vanished along with his fake logistics firm, and while the transaction never went through, proof of its existence and a detailed account of the embezzlement was sent to the FBI, ruining Abbot financially and sending him to jail.

Bart frowned as he read that part of the report. *That's a very obscure company in a fairly low-profile place to be targeted by a scammer. And Whetherby doesn't say there were other companies that were also drawn into the con. Why Abbot?*

His doorbell rang, and Bart put the groceries away, then dinner came so he made a plate for himself and brought the file out to the table to read.

The second case attributed to Ghost Boy had to do with Mason Monroe, a real estate developer also from the Jackson area. Monroe had a checkered background, with some very successful projects, several failed ventures, some question-able insurance claims, and charges of running a Ponzi scheme twenty years ago.

Bart wolfed down chicken fried rice while he read, and his mind spun as he tried to connect the dots.

Monroe had gone to trial on credible allegations of running a real estate scam that promised investors tremen-dous appreciation on tracts of land. The sales pitch had based those projections on the rumors of a new stretch of highway and several large factories coming to the area. Early investors made a killing, but the rest lost their shirts when the rumors turned out to be lies, raising the charges of the venture being a Ponzi scheme. Monroe had skated by on probation and a stern warning after talented lawyers got involved. Local gossip suggested bribes played a role.

So Monroe wasn't a choirboy. That probably made him a lot of enemies.

Monroe, whose religious fervor was part of his brand, claimed that the representative of a megachurch pastor sought him out to put together the purchase of land for a large compound that would include a cathedral, parochial school, and community center. The representative, a man named Carl Dillinger, asked Monroe to front the purchases to keep the true reason for the land purchases quiet and avoid driving up the prices.

Monroe knew the pastor's reputation, so when the repre-sentative asked him to accept the current church buildings as collateral and line up loans, Monroe had complied, agreeing to be the "pass through" to keep the media off the megachurch's trail.

Once the papers were signed and Monroe was on the hook for the loans, it turned out the real pastor and his megachurch didn't know a thing about the transaction, had made no plans—and had no representative named Carl

Dillinger. The media had a field day, and once again, a complete dossier went to the FTC. Monroe's company collapsed under the weight of the loans, he became a laughingstock, and ended up in jail.

Bart pushed away his empty plate, wiped his mouth, and finished his Coke. Whetherby's research was good, but Bart felt certain that the other agent had overlooked something important.

He poured a glass of brandy and got comfortable on the couch to read more. A banker in Humboldt claimed he had been "led astray" under false pretenses by a Hollywood high roller named Ed Fleming who sold him on underwriting a loan to bring movie production—and the money that went with it—to Humboldt. The banker agreed to be the administrator for the loan, writing checks to turn a warehouse into a studio and equip it.

Once the deal was done, someone tipped off the media to find a studio outfitted for shooting pornographic movies, including plenty of BDSM equipment shipped in the banker's name. Fleming disappeared, and the banker's conservative community demanded his immediate resignation, filing charges against him based on a slew of local "indecency" laws.

That case made Bart laugh. *If there really is a single son of a bitch behind this, he's one clever bastard. Everything's done long-distance. No one's caught him on film.*

The most recent fraud attributed to Ghost Boy involved a patrol officer in Medina. The officer was an avid gym rat, and said he was approached by Glen Howell, owner of a supplement company, who wanted to feature him in commercials and make him a distributor for their line of herbal products.

The cop had jumped at the chance for a lucrative side gig, even though it required a "down payment" of several thousand dollars. Endorsements were recorded online and started playing on social media. A large shipment of "protein powder" arrived at his house, which he signed for and stored in his garage.

Then someone tipped off his superiors, who discovered that the "supplements" were laced with Ecstasy. The cop claimed he had been set up, but a jury wasn't sympathetic and sentenced him to prison. The uncashed but incriminating checks were included in the file sent to the state Attorney General.

"Wait a second," Bart mumbled, flipping pages. "It is one guy. Andrew Benchley. Carl Dillinger. Ed Fleming. Glen Howell. A, b, c, d, e, f, g, h—holy hell. That can't be a coincidence. Ghost Boy's a cheeky bastard who can't help 'signing' his work."

He's pulled off some very intricate frauds. There are certainly bigger targets and larger payoffs. The perp didn't walk away with any money for the risk involved. So why these victims?

Bart remembered something a former boss had told him. *If a crime isn't logical, then it's personal.*

This isn't a crime spree—it's a vendetta. Who are you, Ghost Boy, and how did these people earn your wrath?

As Bart went through the notes again, he noticed several things that made him wonder about the previous investigator. While the crimes were recounted in great detail, it didn't look as if Whetherby had done a deep dive into the background of the victims or why they might have been singled out by Ghost Boy.

Bart started a list. Background research on the victims was the first notation. The second item was looking into the relevance of the locations. All the crimes targeted people who lived in small towns not far from Memphis, but that weren't the sort of places to draw notice from folks who weren't from the area. Whetherby was convinced that they had been chosen at random to "test" different kinds of fraud, but that didn't sit right with Bart.

Whetherby seemed to have come at the cases seeing Ghost Boy as a career criminal driven by money and hadn't considered revenge as motivation. That became the third item on Bart's list.

Sure, some people like to see if they can break into a system just to prove it can be done. But they usually flaunt their wins all over the internet. They're in it for attention and to show off their cleverness. That doesn't seem to fit here.

After each fraud, social media accounts had revealed the guilt of the people who had been targeted. Those accounts turned out to be fake names set up on public Wi-Fi—untraceable. As Bart scanned pages of screen captures, he noticed that none of the posts vaunted the skill of the thief. All of them focused on wrongdoing by the marks, reducing sympathy and suggesting they had it coming.

Bart made a note to look at those details closer. He referenced the Tennessee map where Whetherby had marked the locations of the fraud victims. The towns weren't far apart—which made Bart wonder if Ghost Boy lived somewhere nearby.

He eyed the list of targets again. Show-offs usually hacked into a government database, compromised a military weapons system, or drained money from accounts. Ghost Boy hadn't acted like a terrorist, or an activist, or even a misguided adventurer. He'd put the spotlight on the people he hit, not on himself.

Bart wondered how many more targets were on Ghost Boy's list, because he had the feeling time to catch their elusive perp was running out. Unless he slipped up, once Ghost Boy got to the end of his enemies list, he was likely to fade away and they'd lose their chance to nab him.

He put his bourbon aside, and went into the bedroom,

retrieving a small, well-worn duffel bag. Bart hadn't planned to put his abilities to work quite so quickly, but this case had gotten its hooks into him, and he knew he'd never sleep if he didn't run down a couple of angles right away.

Bart glanced at the time, then realized that didn't matter. The person he needed would be available.

He pushed the rug aside and chalked a circle on the hardwood floor, including warding sigils on both sides of the line. Bart lit white pillar candles at the quarters. In a small silver bowl, he combined a fragment of one of Whetherby's handwritten notes, along with bay leaf, mugwort, wormwood, and a drop of Bart's own blood.

"Hank Whetherby, I ask you to appear. I would speak to you, but mean you no harm. Appear before me, cause no damage, and I will ease your rest."

Bart sat cross-legged inside the summoning circle with the folder in his lap and waited. A chill in the air grew until he could see his breath, and he sensed a spirit's presence.

"Who the hell are you, and why are you bothering me?" The voice matched the appearance of the shade that formed on the other side of the circle. Whetherby had been in his sixties when he died, with tufts of white hair, sharp dark eyes, and an irascible set to his mouth.

"I'm Bartlett Gibson, TBSI, and I want to talk about the Ghost Boy case."

Whetherby loosed a string of profanity. "Can't even get off the fuckin' job when I die. Make it quick. I don't think I can get overtime here."

That tugged a wan smile to Bart's lips. "I'll be brief. What made you conclude that the perpetrator was practicing for bigger targets?"

Whetherby glared. "Because no one would run cons like that for such shitty payoffs. He stalked those people, knew their weaknesses, and hit them where it hurt the most—

money, reputation, destroying their companies, becoming unemployable. A guy like that is just getting warmed up before he goes for the big time—blackmailing politicians, cracking nuclear codes, hacking into the World Bank."

Bart could see Whetherby's point of view, but he couldn't help feeling that his predecessor had jumped to some conclusions.

"Did you ever pull in one of the profilers to see what they might make of the guy?" TBSI had a few profilers and access to more through the FBI.

Whetherby snorted. "Why waste the money? I spent nearly forty years in law enforcement. It gave me a nose for this kind of thing. I don't need to psychoanalyze the fucker— just need to catch him. Wished I could have done that while I was breathing."

Bart had learned the futility of arguing with the dead, so he remained silent. Whetherby's derisive tone solidified the gut feeling that had tugged at the edges of his mind as he read over the man's notes. He'd seen it in others, both cops and agents, and it didn't always correlate with age.

When the perp stops being a person with a motive and becomes a villain with a cause, presuppositions get in the way of good fieldwork.

"Did you have any theories you didn't put in the file?" Bart added some things to his follow-up list for later.

"I think the guy is a psychopath who gets off on manipulating people and destroying them," Whetherby said, his voice far from neutral. His tone made it clear he despised Ghost Boy and wanted to see him punished.

What is it about these cases that jerks Whetherby's chain? Because something's triggered him.

"Did you know any of the victims? I get the feeling that these cases struck close to home for you," Bart probed.

"I didn't know any of them personally, but I grew up

around people like them. Hard-working folks who made a mistake or two along the way. But they put in the time and built something from nothing, and then some smartass punk comes in and wipes away their lifetime's worth of work." Whetherby's ghost sneered.

"Maybe they weren't as upstanding as they seemed," Bart suggested.

"See, that's where everything goes wrong these days. People have to be goddamn fucking saints, or nothing they do counts. Nobody gets the benefit of the doubt. You gotta look at the whole picture."

He knows something, and it set him off. Something he doesn't want to admit.

"When you looked into the victims, did you find out about things they might have done in the past that were illegal...unethical...or just downright not neighborly?"

Bart wasn't a profiler, but he had learned a lot about reading people's expressions. As a necromancer, he was acutely aware of the ghost's energy. That wasn't the same as being able to read thoughts, but Bart could pick up on the shifts in the frequency of the energy to indicate strong emotions.

"Don't tell me I got replaced by one of those fucking do-gooders," the ghost snarled. "Why don't you save time and just lock everyone up? We've all done bad things—but when someone does good, it cancels out the bad. Digging up the past doesn't serve anything."

Except for the people who never got justice. The ones who didn't have the power or the voice to be heard. And burying the sins of the past without acknowledging them means the same things will just keep happening.

Bart didn't want to know what Whetherby's long-ago transgressions had been, but the ghost was arguing too hard for absolution of the sort he seemed to want for himself.

"You make sure you nail that bastard, you hear?" Whetherby insisted.

Bart was glad he'd never met his predecessor in person. "I'll do my best to make sure that everyone involved gets what they deserve," he replied. "Go in peace."

Whetherby's image faded and vanished. The room grew warmer, and Bart blew out all but one of the candles. He used the last one to burn the items in the silver bowl to ash. Later, he'd bury what remained on holy ground. He released the energy he had gathered, thanked the elements, and washed away the chalk marks with a mix of vinegar and water.

Necromancers didn't decide a spirit's afterlife, although they could speed their passage to wherever they were bound. Bart didn't believe in heaven or hell—at least not in the popular versions people had shaped from lore and literature. From what he'd observed, and the nature of the eternal energies that he felt around him, he leaned more toward believing in a cycle of refinement until a soul had learned and grown. Ghosts that hung onto resentments and rage after death usually had a long path to walk.

Does the director buy into Whetherby's theory, or is he just trusting an agent to do good research and come to solid conclusions? How much guff will I get if I throw the whole thing out and start over?

Bart didn't actually need to start from scratch. But he had already decided not to accept Whetherby's insights as a foregone conclusion. One of the first things they learned in training was that "bias equals blindness." From Whetherby's heated reaction, the Ghost Boy case had definitely triggered bias, which had kept the late agent from evaluating all the possibilities.

Bart yawned and stretched, feeling the day's activities in every muscle. He'd packed his car the previous day in Nashville, driven several hours to Memphis, and moved into his apartment before going out to check the neighborhood and celebrate a last night of freedom prior to taking on a new case.

Today, he'd met his new boss, acquired groceries and dinner, studied the case, and summoned a surly ghost. While it wasn't terribly late, Bart felt like he'd done enough for one day.

He sipped his bourbon and played through a level of his current video game to make sure everything was hooked up right, but the game didn't hold his attention.

While he wanted to dig deeper into the case, Bart knew it would be better to lay it aside and come back with fresh eyes tomorrow, especially since he would need resources available during regular business hours to follow up on his hunches.

A hot shower sounded like a great idea. Bart knocked back the rest of his drink, closed up for the night and checked the locks, then headed for the bathroom.

Strong water pressure pounded his tight shoulders and sore back. He dropped his head and let rivulets run through his hair before a quick shampoo. His favorite soap with its woodsy smell of cedar and sandalwood helped to relax him.

Bart's thoughts drifted to the previous night. He didn't make a habit of frequenting gay bars—too much of a risk given his job. Still, he was new in town and wanted to burn off some energy, celebrate a little before buckling down to a new assignment. He had heard about Haggarty's and decided to check it out. No harm in looking, even if the cards were stacked against him ever finding a real relationship.

He had only planned to have a drink and do some people watching, get some fresh images for his spank bank. Then he had spotted the ginger at the bar. Something about the stranger had pressed all of Bart's buttons, from the man's build to his casual humor, to the way he really didn't seem to care whether he got lucky.

Taking someone back to his apartment was definitely out, and Bart didn't want to risk a motel. But some quick and dirty fun in the restroom was just what he needed to take the edge off his nerves. The ginger must have liked what he saw because it didn't take long until they were in each other's space, grinding against one another like teenagers, hard cocks finding delicious friction wrapped together in Bart's large hand.

He had memorized the man's scent—orange and clove—the color of his green eyes, the copper of his shaggy hair and scruffy beard. Even more, Bart had concentrated on the sense memory of the heft of the stranger's body against his own, solid, strong, broad-shouldered, and just a few inches shorter.

Bart's hand fell to his now-hard cock, remembering how it had felt to lean into the stranger, cage him against the wall with his arms, knowing that this man was permitting him that illusion of control and could most likely kick his ass. He had warned against making marks—too dangerous for the job—and made it clear he didn't kiss on the lips. At least, not since Shawn.

Bart came hard, letting his release spill over his soapy fist, holding himself up against the tile with his other arm. He worked himself through the aftershocks, still focused on the sense memory of the stranger until he was completely spent.

I wish I dared go back for seconds. Would he be there if I went looking for him? In another reality, could we be more to each other than a one-night stand?

He ended the shower and toweled off, pulling on soft sweats and a worn T-shirt. Sleep came quickly, bringing with it dreams of a handsome man with dark curly hair and deep brown eyes, matching gold rings, motorcycles, blood, death, and heartbreak.

Bart woke with a gasp, fighting his way out of the tangled sheets. His heart pounded, and sweat soaked his shirt.

Funny how four years melted into nothing, leaving only heartache as fresh as in the first few moments after loss. Bart's fist gripped his wet shirt over his heart, struggling to breathe against the pain.

He remembered that night in excruciating detail, from the phone call about the hit and run to the smell of Shawn's blood mingled with the antiseptic odor of the hospital, the beep of the machines, the eternity waiting for answers.

Worse, when the answers came. Bart remembered how still and pale Shawn looked in the hospital bed beneath the wires and breathing tube. How patiently the doctor explained the extent of brain damage and irreversible paralysis, how the machines could keep his heart beating, but Shawn would never wake up.

Worse, as a witch and necromancer, Bart knew the doctor was right. Technically, he could resurrect the dead—but Shawn's mind and body were broken beyond repair. If Shawn's body hadn't been so badly damaged, Bart could have used his power to anchor Shawn's soul—if he had wanted to stay—and keep him alive beyond medical measures while he healed. He could have bent his magic to enhancing what science could do, speeding healing and limiting pain.

But Shawn's body and brain wouldn't ever heal right. Bart's magic couldn't fix that magnitude of damage, and tethering his soul would have been beyond cruel.

Bart had seen Shawn's soul standing beside his broken body. At least his gift permitted them a chance to say goodbye, and for Bart to make Shawn's passing quick and painless, easing his path to what lay beyond. Shawn didn't want to stay as a ghost, and Bart wouldn't ask him to do so, even though he had the power to keep them together like that. He had seen Shawn's soul cross the Veil, felt his energy pass beyond, and knew the parting was final.

Afterward, Bart moved the gold ring on Shawn's right hand to his left, where it would have gone on their wedding day, and buried him with that bleak fulfillment. Bart hung his ring from a chain around his neck, reminding him of the oath he made by Shawn's bedside to bring his killer to justice.

In the days that followed, Bart had used his training and connections to investigate when the police proved disinterested. Everything pointed to a state senator with a history of driving drunk. Shawn's family was intimidated out of pursuing the case, and since he and Shawn weren't married, Bart didn't have legal standing to fight on his own.

So Bart took matters into his own hands. He found the ghosts of the senator's other victims and witnesses who eagerly told him their stories and helped him document his case. Then he empowered the ghosts to haunt the man, harrying him to distraction. Bart sent his evidence anonymously to an investigative reporter, and when the story made the headlines, the haunting had already broken the senator's will and made him question his sanity. He confessed, destroying his political career.

That victory didn't bring back Shawn or heal the hole in Bart's heart. Perhaps it saved other lives. But Bart had the cold satisfaction of stopping someone who had been above the law and holding him accountable for his crimes. He set aside the ring and the chain in a box, vengeance fulfilled.

As the pain and memories receded, Bart thought of the thick folder in the living room documenting Ghost Boy's crimes. The odd itch in the back of his brain now made him wonder.

Revenge ties the cases together much better than Whetherby's theory. So if I want to find Ghost Boy, I need to dig into the sins of the past and figure out who the fraud victims hurt. When I find the person they all have in common, I'll find Ghost Boy.

If I'm right and he's after justice the system failed to give him, what do I do if I catch him?

CHAPTER THREE

RJ

Two days later, RJ waited in line at a coffee shop near a large office park. He had decided to treat himself since the Carmody job had been a success. The news sites and television coverage had a heyday with the corrupt foster parents. And while he knew his former caregivers wouldn't be carried off in shackles just yet, RJ felt some weight lift from his shoulders knowing they were finally going to be held accountable.

"Fancy meeting you here," a familiar voice rumbled. Tall Guy was in line behind him, looking just as scrumptious as he had at Haggerty's.

"Well, hello there." RJ grinned. "Need a caffeine hit?"

The man rolled his eyes heavenward. "So bad you wouldn't even believe it." He returned the smile. "You getting that to go, or do you have time to drink it here?"

"I'm all for being sociable," RJ said as the barista handed off his cup.

Tall Guy's order was done minutes later, and they

selected an out-of-the-way table where the busy café wasn't too loud.

"I'm Bart," Tall Guy said as they sat.

"Jon." RJ used the alias that had served him well for so long.

"You got a haircut and shaved off the beard," Bart noted.

RJ's hair was back to ginger but shorter than the mop he'd had when he and Bart met. He sported a couple of days' reddish stubble, different from his full beard.

"Job interview," he lied. "Needed to be a little less scruffy."

Bart gave him a knowing glance. "There's something to be said for scruff."

His voice pitched low so no one else could hear him, and the tone went right to RJ's groin. He shifted in his seat and saw a glint in Bart's eyes that told him the other man knew he was getting to RJ.

We really can't end up fucking in the coffee shop bathroom, RJ told himself. *For one thing, it's a single-user, and there'd be no excuse for two of us in there together.*

"Maybe if I get hired, I can grow it back," RJ replied.

Bart shrugged. "You look good either way."

RJ cleared his throat, pleased but not wanting to blush. "Nice to see we're both coffee-holics." It was the safest topic he could think to broach.

"I'm sure it will catch up to me, eventually. But until then…" He let his voice drift off as he took another drink.

RJ couldn't help watching the way the man's Adam's apple bobbed as he swallowed and the muscles in the elegant line of his neck. White foam lingered on Bart's lips, and he swiped his tongue to lick it away, giving RJ a knowing look.

Damn him. He knows exactly what effect he has.

Bart laughed, easing the tension. He relaxed in his chair, cluing RJ that he'd been teasing. "So…seen any good movies lately?"

Back on safer ground, RJ could breathe again. "Not as many as I'd like, but I try to catch up when they come on streaming. You?"

"Crazy work hours. I binge-watch when I get a break."

They spent the next half hour chatting about everything and nothing. The potent attraction sizzled beneath the surface, but neither of them acted on it. RJ found himself enjoying the first real conversation he'd had in a long time that wasn't a transaction with a clerk or a setup with a target.

All too soon, Bart glanced at his watch. "Oops. I need to get back." He paused, then seemed to make up his mind.

"Hey, would you like to do dinner tomorrow night? No strings, no expectations." He hurried to add, and then the hint of a wicked smile quirked the corner of his lips. "Although I'm open to suggestions."

"Sure." RJ surprised himself by answering before his over-cautious brain caught up. "Got a place in mind?"

Bart named a popular barbecue joint. "I'm new in town, so I haven't been there, but I've heard it's good."

"It's legit. If you like 'cue, you'll love it."

"Let's say seven." Bart stood. "Sorry to dine and dash, but duty calls. See you tomorrow night."

He was out the door before RJ realized that they hadn't traded phone numbers.

Well, we traded names this time. And while the guy is hot as hell, he can also carry on a conversation. Nice to know.

Wait—did I just agree to go on a date? Bad idea. I can't afford to get distracted. I'm too close to the finish line.

But...what could it hurt? I'm not going to take him home with me. We might not even fuck, although that would be a shame.

It's just been a long time since I actually talked to someone. I won't let it cause a problem. I'm not even going to be in town much longer. But it's a nice fantasy. And now I've got a name to go with the face. Bart.

He felt a little bad about giving the man an alias, even though "Jon Miller" had been his legal name since not long after he'd fled the Carmodys. It hid him from pursuit, but in his heart, he never stopped being Ricky Jon.

We'll have a little fun, and then I'll leave town, and it'll be over. He's sex on legs, funny, interesting, and can carry a conversation. I'm going to enjoy the hell out of this while I can...collect some good memories.

He finished his now-cold latte, tossed the cup in the trash, and caught himself humming as he walked back to his car parked by the library. RJ had come into town to research, and for a break from his motel room. He looked around at the office buildings on every side and wondered where Bart worked, what a guy like that did for a living.

Short hair—banking? Finance? Insurance? He's out of my league, but for as long as this is going to last, I'm going to enjoy trading up.

He spent an hour using the library Wi-Fi and headed back to his motel, still flying a little from his encounter with Bart.

RJ switched motels every week, sticking to the outskirts of Memphis. Plenty of tourists came and went, so he could fade into the background. Sunglasses, a baseball cap, and a health mask thwarted most facial recognition programs for any cameras he couldn't avoid when he was working a job to bring down another target. Cash paid for everything, untraceable. He had been saving up for the chance to put things right for a long, long time.

The thrill of being on the run had faded long ago. To keep his spirits up between targets, RJ had found a few things that worked over the two years of his "vengeance tour." Plenty of state parks within a short drive let him hike and enjoy the outdoors in freedom with a low chance of being spotted or pursued. He found a couple of discount movie theaters and a drive-in that offered distraction beyond what motel cable provided. He'd already been to the zoo, botanical garden, and aquarium.

Going solo wasn't ideal, but RJ had learned long ago to make do.

His favorite late-summer outings were the food festivals and county fairs that popped up every weekend. RJ didn't go for the rides, which he skipped entirely. He enjoyed the food —gloriously unhealthy and orgasmically delicious. Then he wandered past the livestock exhibits and 4-H barns, along with the displays of brand-new trucks and RVs. Tractor pulls, dirt track races, and live concerts were worth the price of a ticket, but they weren't what pulled RJ back time after time.

For him, the magic started at sundown, when the fair came alive with lights. White bulbs outlined the buildings and midway booths. Neon accentuated the ride signage, casting everything in its glow, sharpening the divide between light and shadow.

When the lights came on, the tawdriness disappeared, replaced by something shiny and wondrous. In broad daylight, it could be hard to overlook the smell of the barns, the overfilled trash bins, the peeling paint, or signs of disrepair. But at night, under the blaze of the colored bulbs, the world transformed into a swirl of possibility and excitement where RJ could remember better times.

Which is how he found himself at a small fair a few nights later with a corn dog in one hand and a Slurpee in the other. He walked through a building with all the award-winning pies, homemade bread, and amateur art that had brought blue ribbons and a moment of glory to their creators.

A family with three young children navigated the crowds ahead of him. From the back, they could have been his parents with him and his brother and sister in tow. Before the bad things happened. He allowed himself the luxury of following them at a safe distance through the building, remembering and pretending.

That was so long ago.

RJ didn't need a degree in psychology to know why he loved fairs and festivals. His mom and dad had enjoyed taking the kids whenever time permitted, a fun day's outing for the whole family. Ricky Jon and his siblings had ridden rides until they were dizzy, tried their luck on the midway, and gorged themselves on cotton candy, snow cones, and fried candy bars. Longer vacations sometimes included Dollywood, Branson, Nashville, or camping in the Great Smokies. But it was the county fairs that remained golden in RJ's memories.

Later, after things went bad, RJ had turned to fairs for survival. When he ran away from the Carmodys, RJ had been fifteen—not quite legal, but tall enough to pass for older. He had hidden among the tents and trailers of a traveling circus, stealing food. RJ had gotten caught, and the circus master seemed to figure out his situation by his age and the bruises on his arms.

He had started with a job mucking out the stalls and emptying trash—plus three meals, a bunk in one of the wagons, and a paycheck. When the circus moved on, so did RJ. No one found him—but then again, he didn't think anyone had bothered looking.

RJ gradually moved up to better jobs and more pay. The circus master took a shine to RJ and offered him the chance to throw the Carmodys off his trail by assuming the name of his own dead son who would have been close to RJ's age. A few hundred dollars made the switch legal, and RJ had the late child's birth certificate if anyone ever looked closely.

When the circus master realized that RJ had untrained psychic abilities, he landed a spot in the fortune teller tent that got a percentage commission and helped him hone his skills.

His time on the road meant that, unlike most visitors, when RJ walked through a fair or circus, he knew what he was *really* seeing, even though he had never worked for this particular amusement company. He understood the skill it took to handle the trained animals, put up tents and disassemble rides. RJ could spot the pickpockets and the plain-clothes bouncers. He could tell the carnival workers from the local roadies and vendors, and he knew at a glance whether the rides were death traps.

Through the years, there had been good troupes and bad ones. He had stayed with the first company until his mentor retired. After that, sometimes RJ changed carnivals season by season, while he rode with others for a couple of years at a time, embracing what outsiders called the "carny" life and even learning to speak a little of the insider language, Cizarny, from some of the old-timers.

He recognized early on that traveling fairs worked year-round, with a northern and southern route, a way to keep a roof over his head and build up the savings he'd need to carry out the revenge scheme he had dreamed about for most of his life.

Different names and faces, same job and drama.

He finished his corn dog and the last of his Slurpee then got a funnel cake with strawberries and ice cream. The concert had begun, a has-been band with name recognition and a few hits, loud enough to hear outside the grandstand. Teenagers jostled the other pedestrians, bunches of high school girls preening for the attention of the roving gangs of boys trying to look cool. Kids melted down from their sugar rush. Lovers slipped behind the food trucks and exhibit buildings for groping and stolen kisses.

A dark-haired young girl with a ponytail skipped by. RJ

caught sight of her out of the corner of his eye and just for a second, saw Kit, his older sister. A glimpse of a blond, broad-shouldered young man joking with his friends reminded RJ so much of his big brother, Mick, that he had to turn away.

Maybe coming here wasn't a good idea.

RJ took a deep breath and drank in the atmosphere. The distant music from the band mingled with the tinny calliope of the carousel, the shouts of the barkers, and the laughter of the crowd. Smooth vanilla ice cream blended perfectly with the crunch of fried dough in his mouth.

Fuck it. I'm home.

RJ glimpsed two teenage boys pushing and shoving a younger boy behind one of the exhibit buildings. He hesitated for a moment, knowing it was none of his business and that risking getting picked up by the cops at this point would ruin everything.

Seconds later, he followed, keeping to the shadows.

He heard the dull thud of fists on flesh before he could see what was going on. RJ pulled on his health mask and tipped his ball cap lower, then stepped out into the dull light.

"Leave the kid alone and get the fuck out of here," he ordered in his gruffest voice.

The older teens looked up, giving their victim a few seconds' reprieve. They were even younger than he'd first thought, probably under sixteen. "Who's gonna make us? You?" one of them taunted.

RJ had a shiv in his boot, and he knew how to use it, thanks to plenty of fights—large and small—growing up on the road. These punks didn't worry him, but he had no desire to attract attention.

He drew himself up to his full height and squared his shoulders. Working out was one of the ways he kept sane, and he'd layered muscle on his six-foot frame. RJ sauntered toward them, stance loose but ready, telegraphing that he could handle himself.

The two toughs watched him uneasily, torn between saving face and sensing a true threat.

"Fuck it," one of them muttered. "He's not worth it." They ran off, and RJ turned back to the smaller boy who still hunched on the ground, unsure whether he'd been saved or delivered to a worse fate.

"You're safe," RJ told him. "Does that happen a lot?"

The boy looked away, humiliation coloring his cheeks. "Yeah."

"Then you need to get out of here." In the faint light from the midway, RJ figured the boy was around fifteen and doubted there were any parents in the picture.

"And go where?"

"Anywhere but here." RJ pulled a few twenties from his wallet and handed them to the kid, who snatched them away like he feared a trap. "Go, and stay gone. Start over. Good luck."

He walked away and the boy left without looking back. RJ rejoined the hubbub in the midway, acutely aware of how much the kid reminded him of his younger self.

The altercation dimmed his mood, and while he had planned to stay until the music ended and the lights went down, RJ decided to leave. Near the front gate, he saw posters for other area fairs. A lurid broadside for the Carnival of Mysteries caught his eye, reminding him of several horror movies he had watched. *I'll have to check that one out. Looks like my kind of place.* He noted the location and dates, promising himself he would visit soon. *But not tomorrow. I've got a date with Bart.*

RJ wasn't worried about encountering the two punks on his walk to his car, but he palmed his shiv, just in case, and kept his guard up.

RJ couldn't shake his melancholy as he drove back to the motel. The Honeysuckle Inn was too upscale for the drug dealers and the drunks, nice enough for mid-price sex workers and tired truckers. Its neon sign buzzed, and the large flower next to the name flickered.

The room held two queen beds with matching floral bedspreads that coordinated with the trellis print of the wallpaper and the garden motif of the lamps and cheap paintings. No roaches scattered when he flicked on the overhead light —a perk, and not to be taken for granted. The kitchenette had a sink, mini fridge, coffee pot, and microwave. A yellow, flower-patterned Formica-topped table with orange molded plastic chairs sat in a corner, while a cheap television took up most of the dresser. The white subway-tiled bathroom had a shower large enough for him to have elbow room, another plus.

Over the years, RJ felt certain he'd seen just about every motel decorating theme, just like in that show about the monster-hunting brothers.

He poured a drink and watched a rerun of *Road House* on one of the streaming channels, trying to wear himself out so he could fall asleep with a chance of avoiding nightmares. RJ dozed halfway through the Swayze flick, but even the bourbon didn't stop him from waking with a start, barely muffling his cries.

The dream's details were twisted around, but the main event pulled directly from his worst memories, claiming his brother's body after a forklift accident in a shoddy warehouse.

Mick had been seventeen, and thirteen-year-old RJ had gone with Kit, just fifteen herself, to identify Mick's body since the Carmodys couldn't be bothered. Even at that age, RJ suspected that Mick's death could have been prevented if corners hadn't been cut, but no one was going to listen to a couple of orphans. He and Kit had no money and the Carmodys weren't about to spend a dime, so Mick had been buried in the public cemetery in an unmarked grave.

RJ swiped the back of his hand over his eyes, wiping away tears. Mick had been dead now longer than he'd been alive, and RJ figured he was probably the only person who remembered his quick humor and wide smile. The job that cost Mick his life had been under the table, which helped him keep both the position and his meager earnings a secret from the Carmodys, who would have felt entitled to his wages on top of the state stipend for his care.

"When I'm eighteen, I'll get kicked out of the system," Mick had told RJ and Kit. *"If I have a job and a place to live, I can petition to get you and Kit away from Mr. Joss. And if not, we'll all run away together."*

But Mick died, and then Kit ran away the next year, promising to send for RJ once she found work. He never heard from her again. Alone and preferring any fate to remaining with his foster parents, RJ disappeared a year later.

That was long ago, but the dreams made it feel like yesterday. RJ ran a hand through his hair, trying to slow his breathing and regain control.

Just one more job—for Mick—and I'm done. Gotta keep my eye on the prize.

A glance at the clock told him it was three in the morning. He lay back down and got comfortable, doing his best to rest if not sleep, drifting off for a few restless hours just before dawn.

The next morning RJ showered, made a pot of coffee, and microwaved a breakfast sandwich before venturing out to another of the many public libraries he visited for their Wi-Fi. RJ made sure not to show up to any location too often, switching among them randomly to avoid leaving an easy pattern to follow, using library cards with fake names based on equally false identification. He didn't like to be on the motel's connection for too long either, and staying in the room made him stir crazy.

No one gave him a second look in his cap and tinted glasses. RJ set up in the back row of computers. After the dreams that kept him awake most of the night, RJ began by checking the alerts he set for any sign of Kit. By now, he had exhausted all reasonable possibilities, and he resigned himself to accepting her death, but he still wanted to know when, where, and how. He sighed when the program turned up nothing, as usual.

When I disappear, the only ones who might look for me are the cops.

Next, he couldn't help checking for any updates on Hank Whetherby, the TBSI agent who had been chasing him for the past two years. RJ found it perversely amusing to stalk his stalker, figuring that keeping an eye on the man who had been assigned to run him down was just good sense.

RJ had been too busy to check for news about Whetherby for the past two weeks, preparing for his encounter with the Carmodys. He gasped when his first search turned up an obituary.

"Holy shit," RJ murmured, then glanced around guiltily at his language, given his location.

Whetherby's dead. I wonder if I pushed him over the edge.

The details of the obit confirmed what RJ had sussed out from various sources. Whetherby had been a career agent decorated for his service. The write-up didn't name a wife or children, citing a sister as his only survivor. There hadn't been a memorial service, and the place of interment wasn't mentioned. A note at the end suggested that donations be made to a fund for the families of agents killed in the line of duty.

RJ sat back, feeling oddly upset by the news. He had eluded Whetherby for two years and gained a grudging respect for the agent. RJ had also made sure to sow plenty of false trails and red herrings to keep Whetherby occupied. That had been disturbingly easy to do, especially when the "evidence" RJ provided aligned with the persona he created.

Untraceable social media accounts hinted at "test runs" before moving on to "bigger things." He seeded just enough vague comments laced with a general dislike of the current state of the world to give the older man fodder for conspiracy theories. The more time Whetherby spent searching for RJ among the disaffected riffraff, the less effort he was putting into anticipating RJ's next move.

I wonder who took over for him. Whoever it is won't have to worry about me for much longer—I'm almost done, and I'll be out of their hair forever.

RJ checked out the library's paperback sale, picking up a stack of books for a few dollars, and then ran some errands before going back to the motel. A ham and cheese sandwich, coffee, chips, and cookies made an adequate lunch.

His pile of mystery and fantasy books gave him something to look forward to, a fresh change from the many public domain books he had downloaded. When he was finished with them, he would drop them in various donation boxes, making it more difficult for anyone to connect them to him or go looking for fingerprints.

Before he left the circus circuit, a friend had helped him set up a laptop that would be virtually untraceable as long as RJ took precautions like using encryption and sticking to either public Wi-Fi or VPNs to hide his location. Even so, he liked to spread his research out by using library computers to muddy his tracks.

The laptop was a godsend when it came to ebooks and free courses. The Carmodys claimed to be homeschoolers, but it was just a disguise for truancy. Mick and Kit taught RJ to read, and he devoured any books he could get his hands on. Whenever he could get access, he watched video classes on everything and anything. The programs scratched an insatiable itch for knowledge and enabled him to carry on a conversation like an educated person.

RJ—or rather, Jon Miller—earned an online degree in pre-law, and he took all the paralegal courses he could find to help him prepare for the day he would call to account the people who had destroyed his loved ones. He'd made good grades, graduated with honors, and wished he could have celebrated with his family.

RJ pushed his empty plate away and sighed. *God I'm tired of running. I just want this to be over, to see some justice done, and then fade away into the sunset—hopefully, on a beach.*

He had picked up skills with the circus, like being a short-order cook, working with machinery, and doing construction, jobs that could earn some extra money and keep him from running through his savings too quickly once he left the circuit. The money he had stashed in offshore accounts should keep him comfortable for a long time once he finished his vendetta, but it eased his mind to know he could rustle up cash if needed.

And in a pinch, there was always poker and pool, more skills honed from a life on the road.

RJ's vision blurred, graying out. *Oh, fuck no. Not now.*

The vision only lasted seconds, a close-up of a man's face, someone RJ had never seen before. A round-faced, portly, white, middle-aged man with dark hair appeared in his mind as if he were only inches away. Nothing about the stranger was remarkable except for his eyes. The cold malice in the man's gaze made RJ shiver, and his heart thudded as he felt them focus on him.

As quickly as it came, the vision had ended, leaving RJ

hyperventilating at the table, dry-mouthed with panic, gripping the edge white-knuckled. He swallowed down the rest of his coffee, and his hand shook as he gripped the cup.

Who the hell was that? Why is he important? He's not familiar, so maybe I haven't met him yet. Whoever he is, this can't be good. I got the distinct impression he's not a fan.

RJ took a few deep breaths to calm himself, then pushed down his qualms, grabbed the drug store bag, and headed into the bathroom, giving himself a critical once-over in the mirror.

Shorter hair and no beard certainly changed his look somewhat from that night at Haggerty's, but he was still recognizable. After dying his hair dark for his meeting with the Carmodys—the only one of his marks he met with in person—he had gone back to his natural ginger.

After his date with Bart tonight, RJ was going blond to disguise himself before he infiltrated his next target's company.

The choice to meet Joss Carmody face to face after all this time had been emotional, not logical. RJ knew it could cost him, but he needed to look the man who had made his childhood a living hell in the eye one last time.

He had been so careful to avoid having his picture taken or being caught on film, but RJ knew Carmody could probably describe him well enough to a police sketch artist. On the other hand, without a photo in the system, there wouldn't be anything to match, just like with his fingerprints.

It was too late to beat himself up over risking exposure, but the possibilities made RJ twitchy. There were still a couple of days before Carmody was likely to realize he'd been scammed. If he could just assemble everything he needed for his last con before then, RJ could leave Tennessee in his rearview mirror, making his way to the Maldives—

where there was no extradition—through a series of moves he had already planned.

RJ sat down with the folder he had put together on his final target. Herbert Osterman ran a warehouse in Jackson near Interstate 40. Companies paid to store their products until they were ready to ship. Osterman's operation received the pallets from the incoming transportation and loaded them onto the outgoing trucks.

Mick had been crushed when another employee lost control of the forklift he'd been driving—underage. When RJ dug into Osterman Freight's history, he found a long list of alleged safety violations and injury lawsuits that magically disappeared thanks to friendly local politicians and judges. There were even some credible allegations that Osterman was smuggling drugs among the many cargo crates in his warehouse.

It had taken RJ more than a year to collect the evidence and carefully document infractions. There couldn't be any doubt that the warehouse played fast and loose with the rules. But without accountability, Osterman had no reason to change, especially when improvements cut into profits.

Now, he had a lengthy list of workers who had been hurt or killed on the job in Osterman's employ. RJ suspected the true toll was higher since he figured some workers either didn't report their injuries or might not show up in the system if they were undocumented.

He had also compiled a record of every OHSA complaint Osterman ignored, every politician whose campaign he donated to, and which companies did business with his warehouse. And as with the Carmody case, RJ had quietly cultivated a social media connection under a false identity to connect with a muckraking reporter who had a record for exposing corruption, who would eventually get a copy of all of RJ's evidence.

After a few hours and a second cup of coffee, RJ stretched and heard the plastic chair creak with his motion. He took a break, getting a cup of chili at a nearby diner. He was already looking forward to meeting Bart for dinner. The barbecue place where they were going was one of RJ's favorites. More than once he had picked up a pulled pork sandwich with onion rings, cole slaw, macaroni and cheese, house-made pickles, and peach cobbler, along with a half-gallon of sweet tea. The food never disappointed.

And whether or not he got lucky, he knew that tonight the company would be good.

RJ ate his chili while he looked over his notes, and then pulled up street view images of the warehouse, checking it out from one angle and then another. He mapped out his route as well as several alternates, and picked a place to park where he could have easy access while keeping his car from being readily noticed.

Despite all his research into the shady warehouse's operations, RJ wanted to make sure the case against Osterman was watertight. So during the overnight shift, RJ intended to add another component—video.

He had already scoped out the building with a few walks past on different days, unsurprised to find lax security among its many failings. RJ noted the way workers dressed and had picked up the dark shirt, reflective vest, and black pants that were the norm. Few of the employees wore hard hats, although a smattering used health masks, which made RJ's plan easier.

But first, reckless as it might be, RJ had a date.

He knew he was fussing too much over his hair—manicuring his stubble and manscaping— but it had been a long time since there'd been anyone to notice, and he was going to make the most of it.

RJ wore his best shirt, a russet one that complemented his

hair and warmed his pale complexion. Together with a new pair of jeans and a pair of Timberlands that were a rare splurge, he knew he cleaned up well.

He drove to Rosco's Barbecue and parked, then realized his palms were sweating as he gripped the steering wheel.

It's just dinner, he told himself. But nobody had ever made him feel like Bart did.

He grew up fast on the circuit surrounded by roustabouts and wranglers who didn't follow convention and largely lived outside the restrictions of polite society. RJ had plenty of boyfriends and lovers over the years. Those in the carnival life rarely expected permanence, and relationships seldom lasted more than a season.

Moving from place to place had been a necessary distraction in those years. He hadn't wanted more than temporary connections since he still mourned the people he had loved and lost. The dream of vengeance had sustained him, and for a long time, that was enough.

But now, with the end of his quest in sight, RJ found himself wanting more. Maybe he could never tell a partner everything about his old life and the recompense he had dealt out, but perhaps he didn't need to live in self-imposed solitude.

After all, people in WITSEC get married. This isn't too much different.

God, I've got the cart before the horse. We haven't even fucked properly, and I'm picking out china patterns. It's just dinner. And maybe a blow job if I play my cards right.

He went inside and looked for Bart. When he didn't see the tall man waiting, his stomach tightened, fearing he had been stood up.

Bart came in a moment later, looking harried. "Sorry. Work ran over. Have you been here long?" He looked like he really cared whether RJ had been worried.

RJ relaxed and gave a broad smile. "Just got here myself." His stomach growled. "It smells so good in here, and I'm starving."

They followed the hostess to a table. RJ saw Bart slip her a twenty to get a spot out of the thick of the fray. Rosco's did a booming business, with food that deserved the buzz.

"Did you have a good day?" Bart asked after they had ordered. RJ thought it was charming that Bart seemed flustered.

Maybe he's as out of practice as I am.

Their conversation picked up right where it had left off. Despite their chemistry, RJ was in no hurry, fine with a meal and good company, even if nothing else happened between them.

He couldn't remember the last time—if ever—that had been the case. Usually, if pleasantries were observed at all, it was a rushed veneer of politeness before getting down to business, preferably somewhere dark and private.

They talked about shows and books, a shared love of country music and role-playing video games, and admitted without judgment to not being sports fanatics. Bart was a good conversationalist, a rare skill. Usually, RJ found men who either talked incessantly about themselves or kept responses to single syllables.

They clicked in a way that felt effortless, and RJ let himself fully enjoy the moment. *Maybe I can't keep him, but I think I would if I could.*

The thought surprised RJ, who had taken pains not to let any emotional entanglements slow him from his goal. Although he suspected that he and Bart would be combustible in bed, he glimpsed the kind of partnership that might include quiet evenings and long walks, companions as well as lovers.

He didn't know how much he actually wanted that future

until the thought surfaced with a power that scared him. *Just enjoy the moment. Take it one day at a time.*

The evening passed far too quickly. They couldn't linger too long in the busy restaurant, and if they dined together again RJ was tempted to pick a spot with slower service just to keep from being rushed.

"Walk you out?" Bart asked, a courtesy RJ didn't expect. He felt oddly flattered and nodded. They bumped shoulders as they exited together, and RJ wished they dared link hands, but that was out of the question.

"That's yours? Sweet ride," RJ said when he saw the sleek black Corvette Stingray.

Bart grinned with pride. "She's a beauty, isn't she? I travel a lot, so that's what I have instead of a house and a yard with a pool."

"No disagreement from me on that. I've been something of a nomad most of my life too."

The sports car was parked at the edge of the lot near the shadows. Bart nodded toward the darkness, and they stepped away from the overhead lights. RJ stepped closer, and Bart tugged him forward into a kiss.

I guess he's ready to break that rule.

What began as a chaste brush of lips turned hungry and open-mouthed, devouring.

Bart pulled back. "Want to get a room?"

When RJ hesitated, Bart went on. "We don't have to stay all night. I've got an early day tomorrow too. But we could if you're interested."

"God, yes." RJ leaned forward and kissed him again, making it clear that he was in favor of whatever Bart had in mind.

"I saw a place about a mile back," Bart said. His blown pupils and flushed skin gave him a wild look that stoked RJ's hunger. "I'll check in and wait outside for you."

RJ nodded, hardly believing they were going to take this further. "I'll follow you."

Bart led them to a small motel, a mom-and-pop place that was a bit nicer than where RJ was staying. Bart drove up toward the office. RJ found a parking space in the shadows and backed in, out of habitual caution, making it difficult to see his license plate. He had made sure to splash some mud on the tag before meeting up for diner. He had no reason to mistrust Bart, but as much as he liked the man, RJ didn't really know him.

RJ was jogging back to the front of the complex as Bart came from the office. He followed him into one of the rooms and pulled the drapes shut before Bart flicked on the lights.

The room was clean, with a hint of pine, clearly tailored toward tourists on a budget with a hokey country music theme. Framed album covers passed for art, and a wallpaper border of guitars continued the theme. The lamps were boot-shaped.

RJ and Bart looked at each other and burst out laughing. "Well, this is memorable," RJ said.

Bart was in his space faster than RJ expected. "I hope it will be—and not just for the décor." Bart's voice was husky.

Suddenly, RJ felt uncertain. He liked Bart, and he also knew he was lying to the man, who seemed like a decent guy, the sort who deserved to find a forever lover.

I don't want to hurt him.

It's just sex.

Maybe he doesn't see it that way.

Fuck around and find out.

RJ turned off his upstairs brain and leaned in for another molten hot kiss. He wasn't used to having to stretch up to kiss a lover, and the new sensation just made everything *more.*

Bart's hands rested gently on RJ's shoulders, then slid down his arms. One hand moved to the front of his shirt.

"This okay?" Bart growled, making unbuttoning slow and seductive.

RJ's hands dropped to Bart's belt. "Is this?" He dared raise his face to stare into Bart's eyes, seeing a reflection of his own lust and affection that made his stomach swoop.

Bart's slow, sexy smile made RJ's heart pound. "Oh, yeah."

"Just so you know, I'm negative," RJ murmured next to Bart's ear.

"Me, too."

They toed out of their shoes and kept kissing as hands fumbled with fasteners, soon leaving a pile of clothing on the floor, all but their briefs. Bart traced over RJ's chest, pausing to toy with his nipples before sliding down to settle on his hipbones. RJ's hands slid around to Bart's muscled back and then lower to palm his tight ass.

"What do you want?" Bart rumbled as they moved together toward the bed.

"Anything," RJ whispered, and meant it. They might only get one night together, but RJ already knew it was going to be the best he'd ever had.

"I liked your hair longer." Bart's breath ghosted over RJ's neck. "Something to hold onto."

"Want to see you." RJ tugged at the waistband of Bart's briefs.

"Then look." Bart slipped his hands down RJ's hips and beneath the elastic, pushing his down as RJ did the same. "Damn, I can't wait to feel you."

RJ let his fingers trace over Bart's long, hard cock.

"Wait." RJ fished a couple of packets of lube out of the pocket of his jeans.

Bart raised an eyebrow. "Counting on getting lucky?"

RJ gave him a sinful smile. "Hoping to."

They tumbled onto the bed, a delicious tangle of arms and legs, exploring bare skin with hands, lips, and tongues. RJ loved the scrape of Bart's stubble against his belly and the coarse texture of Bart's dark body hair as they slid together.

RJ rolled them over so he was on top, surprising the bigger man who didn't fight it. "I want to blow you." RJ watched the color rise in Bart's face as his eyes widened.

He didn't wait for an answer. Instead, he slipped off the end of the bed, drawing Bart with him until Bart's knees bent at the end of the mattress, and RJ knelt between his legs on the floor.

Most of RJ's liaisons had been hurried and anonymous, rushed encounters in the shadows behind a tent or a bar, accompanied by the smell of piss and garbage. They were fraught with danger, which leveled up the tension but left no chance to savor the moment. For years, that was all RJ knew, and he didn't dare dream of more.

By comparison, this was nearly domestic. A clean, safe room, a partner he had begun to get to know and care about, time to take and give pleasure. RJ tried not to think about how much those changes meant to him, or how he never wanted to let it go, and tried to stay in the here and now.

He looked up with a knowing smile and licked his lips, making sure Bart was watching, before he went to work on his partner's long, thick cock. The catch in Bart's breath and the tremor that went through his body drove RJ on, thoroughly exploring the veins and rigid shaft with his tongue as one hand slipped farther back to roll heavy balls in his palm.

"Yes," Bart gasped, and RJ saw that his fists clenched the sheets as he strained not to buck up into RJ's mouth.

RJ took him down to the root in one gulp. It had been a while, but on this at least, muscle memory didn't fail him. Bart sat up, running his hand lightly through RJ's shorter hair, combing it back with his fingers, and giving a light tug that sent lightning to RJ's straining cock.

RJ gave him his best effort, wet, sloppy, and messy, just like RJ liked to receive, knowing when to hollow his cheeks and suck, when to add friction with his other hand, and how to push his thumb into the bundle of nerves just below the head. From Bart's reaction, RJ figured he was doing a good job.

He used the mingled spit and pre-come to slick a finger and slide it along Bart's taint, pressing just so to tease his p-spot, then circling his rim. Maybe they'd do anal and maybe they wouldn't, but he wanted to hit Bart's prostate and send him flying over the edge.

Something to remember me by.

RJ's left hand dropped from Bart's cock to grip his own aching and neglected prick, giving it a couple of tugs before Bart's grip on his hair tightened, just shy of painful.

"Leave that for me. Want to return the favor." Bart's whiskey-rough voice and his promise nearly made RJ lose it right then, but he doubled down on sucking that fine dick in front of him with everything he had.

Seconds later, Bart came, filling RJ's mouth, dribbling out of the corner of his lips. RJ swallowed what he could and made a show of licking the rest away like a cat with cream, which made Bart's spent cock twitch.

"My turn."

Before RJ realized what was happening, Bart lifted him and pulled him onto the bed, impressive since RJ wasn't a small man. He'd usually been the larger partner in his past pairings, and being manhandled by someone bigger and stronger added a thrill RJ didn't realize he'd been missing.

He didn't have time to catch his breath before Bart had his lips on RJ's cock, licking and sucking with frantic, almost desperate need.

Bart's fingertips ran lightly over RJ's skin with a tenderness—an almost reverence—that surprised RJ. He'd fantasized about this moment since that night at Haggarty's, but dream Bart had been rough and ready, and RJ wasn't sure he knew what to do with this glimpse of vulnerability.

"Bart..." RJ couldn't reach his partner's hair, and Bart's arm kept him pinned on his back so he couldn't sit up.

"So close," RJ murmured, wishing he could watch and knowing it would push him off the cliff. "Just like that. Don't stop. Bart—"

He came hard, feeling his climax build from deep in his belly, crashing through him and short-circuiting his brain.

For just a second, his vision went white and he could have sworn he felt Bart's presence in his mind as well as in the mouth on his cock.

Bart kept bobbing and licking until RJ's softening prick grew too sensitive, and he tried to shuffle away.

He crawled back up on the bed, pulling RJ with him until they lay face to face.

"That was...pretty amazing." RJ was surprised that he felt a little shy in the afterglow. He was used to lovers who walked off—sometimes before reciprocating—or rolled out of bed and hurried away. Waking up beside the man he'd fucked the night before didn't happen often, and those pairings hadn't lasted long.

This is dangerous. I'm in too deep. I'm feeling too much too soon. I should put an end to this.

But he wouldn't. *I can't keep him forever, but I want to have this for as long as I can.*

Bart reached out to trace RJ's chin with a finger. "Was that okay? It's been a while...I'm out of practice." The vulnerability in his eyes was real.

RJ pressed their lips together and smiled. "Sorry—it's

going to take a minute for my brain to come back online. That was…intense. In a good way," he hurried to add.

He glimpsed old scars on Bart's arms and chest and wondered about the story behind them. Bart let his finger continue a slow path down RJ's neck, over his collarbone, skirting the faded pink line that had come from a long-ago knife fight. RJ saw questions in Bart's eyes, but they both knew tonight wasn't the time for stories.

"Next time, I want to fuck you properly." Bart's grin promised trouble. "Maybe switch things up."

Next time. He wants more. "I like the sound of that."

"I'd like to see you again," Bart said quietly. "Not just for sex. Don't get me wrong—this," he fluttered his fingers between them, "is pretty fantastic. But I'd like to get to know you better, see what could happen. If you're interested."

Oh, I'm interested. This is crazy, reckless, stupid, and doomed, but I am so very, very interested. "Yes," RJ replied before his brain could catch up. "I'd like that too."

Bart kissed him slow and deep, a promise for later. He pulled back reluctantly. "We'd probably better get cleaned up. I really do have an early morning tomorrow."

"Me, too," RJ said, although he felt certain they had very different agendas awaiting them.

Bart rolled out of bed, went to the bathroom, and came back with a warm, wet washcloth.

"Let me," he murmured, holding RJ's gaze before he wiped away the traces of their come and sweat.

No one's ever done that before. The gesture seemed extraordinarily intimate. RJ wondered why a guy like Bart was still unattached. *Things that seem too good to be true usually are,* a voice in his mind whispered, but he ignored it.

How can I care so much for a man who doesn't even know my real name?

RJ went to use the bathroom, and when he came out, Bart

had put RJ's clothing on the foot of the bed. Bart already had his pants, socks, and shoes on, and his shirt hung open in the front. He still looked good enough to eat and RJ's cock stirred, although at nearly thirty a second round took a little longer to muster.

"I'll take a rain check on what you're thinking." Bart gave a lascivious grin.

RJ found he hadn't lost the ability to blush. "Count on it." RJ gathered up his clothing and went into the bathroom to change and wash up, rinsing his mouth even though he hated to lose the last taste of Bart on his tongue.

"Thank you for tonight," RJ said when he came out, unsure of the etiquette for this stage.

"I'd say the pleasure was all mine, but I'm pretty sure I gave as good as I got." Bart smirked.

RJ cleared his throat. "I'd, uh, better get going. See you?"

"My phone number's in your back pocket," Bart admitted. "Call me."

RJ let himself out and winced when the door clicked shut behind him. It took willpower not to look over his shoulder. He slipped a hand into his pocket and crinkled the paper there.

Somehow Bart must have sensed that RJ needed space and gave it to him despite the heated attraction between them. RJ's psychic sense told him he was safe with Bart, against all logic. *Maybe Bart had a touch of the same*, he thought, *or was just very good at reading people.* If Bart had come on strong, RJ would have balked like a skittish horse.

Instead, Bart gave him loose reins, just like RJ had seen the animal trainers do at the circus, trusting the horse to come to them on its own.

He drove back to his motel, deep in thought, still on an endorphin high from the best sex he'd ever had.

Had he sensed a bit of something *extra* in their connection? RJ had thought so in that instant when he could have sworn he didn't just feel Bart's body but also touched his thoughts.

Wishful thinking, he chided himself. The only other people he had known with abilities were the few fortune tellers at the carnivals that hadn't been outright frauds. RJ had always wondered what it would be like to find a partner who shared his talent. Would it be even better than the tantric sex he'd read about? Could a psychic lover forge a soul bond or at least a deeper connection between their bodies and minds?

RJ suspected such things were the stuff of romance novels and fantasy books, but deep in his heart of heart, he couldn't help wishing.

Enjoy the dreams, but don't believe them, a piece of his mind warned. *Finishing the mission is one thing. Expecting a happy ending is asking too much.*

CHAPTER FOUR

RJ

*W*hen he got back to his motel, RJ made a fresh pot of coffee and settled down at the table, putting Bart's phone number in his wallet for safekeeping. His evening was far from over. He glanced at the clock, checked to see how long until the evening shift change, downed some coffee, and looked over his notes one more time.

It was easier turning his hair blond than it had been to dye it dark. He only hoped that before the next time he saw Bart, he could get his hair close to its normal color.

RJ changed clothes to fit in. He had half a dozen wireless spy cameras he bought online, each smaller than a postage stamp, in a plastic bag in his pocket, along with a latex glove to avoid leaving prints. The cameras could record for more than a full day and stream their output to a burner phone he bought just for that reason and already set up. He figured that given how bad the warehouse's safety record was, six cameras recording for twenty-four hours could pick up a lot of infractions.

If he was lucky, they might validate some of the drug trafficking rumors too.

RJ parked a distance away from the warehouse then headed for the loading dock, head down and his hands jammed into his pockets. He had made a fake laminated badge with a blurry photo of someone else, but no one bothered to check it.

RJ sighed with relief and looked around. He already had locations in mind. All he had to do was avoid notice while he maneuvered into position to place the cameras where they wouldn't likely be noticed and get back out again.

A supervisor shouted for him to stack some pallets. RJ gave a nod and changed direction to head toward where the man pointed, then he shifted his steps as soon as the boss turned away. He put two cameras in the loading dock, one near the forklifts and skids, another near the ladders and dollies. In between placing the devices, he moved boxes like a worker, scoping out where best to put the last two.

He chose spots near the belt and roller conveyors, which he knew were dangerous. RJ had been nonchalant about his movements, but realized that as long as he moved with purpose from one task to another, no one paid much attention.

All the while, RJ studied his surroundings, estimating the number of shift workers and bosses, the kind of cargo stored, and every cut corner and shortcut on safety he saw. The hum of the conveyors and the buzz of electric forklifts reverberated in the big space with its metal walls and concrete floor. If anyone noticed a new guy, they didn't say anything. In fact, the workers barely grunted at each other, and then only if someone got in their way or needed to hand off a tool.

Are there floggings at midnight? What the hell do they do when someone gets written up if everyone's so cowed?

That's when RJ spotted two men on an elevated platform against the wall in the middle of the warehouse. The tall, florid-faced man he recognized as Osterman and felt a flare of anger. Next to him stood the man from RJ's vision, a squat man dressed in a black suit that looked like it should be worn in a funeral home instead of a warehouse.

RJ was too far away to hear their conversation, and the sight of the man in black made him want to get far away and as fast as possible. As Osterman talked, his companion seemed to completely ignore him, squinting intently at the workers bustling back and forth. RJ had no desire to attract the man's notice and quickly stepped behind a tower of pallets, trying to understand why his pulse raced and he'd broken out in a cold sweat.

He took a deep breath to calm himself and reached out with his psychic sense, which was attracted to other special abilities nearby. His gift pinged a silent alarm, the kind of thing he'd only felt before when he was in imminent danger.

Magic. Round Face has some sort of freaky bad magic. Shit. He's a witch.

RJ remembered watching a prison break movie where a searchlight swept the night looking for escapees. The short man's gaze gave him the same feeling, and RJ didn't want to know what would happen if he was spotted. He feared the witch's attention far more than being caught trespassing.

He knew he couldn't remain hidden, so he kept his head down and moved whenever several workers walked from one place to another, hoping to be lost in the crowd. Gradually, RJ made his way toward the door, trying to figure out how to leave before the end of the shift.

He turned sharply, warned by intuition, just as the tower of pallets he had hidden behind swayed and then collapsed like a giant Jenga as people screamed. RJ felt nearly certain at least one person had been close enough to be hurt if they managed to escape being buried underneath the broken wood. Men shouted and workers rushed forward.

RJ seized the moment to slip through the door, staying in the shadows as the warehouse's few watchmen rushed inside. His heart didn't stop thudding until he was outside the gate and back to his car. Once inside, RJ sat and gripped the steering wheel so hard his knuckles turned white. He slowed his breathing and finally stop shaking.

Witnessing the accident was bad, triggering images of Mick's death. The workers had responded swiftly, and RJ suspected their reaction was based more on frequency than training.

But it had been the moon-faced witch that sent a frisson of terror through RJ. He hadn't just picked up on powerful magic; it had been the sheer malice in the energy that chilled him to the core.

Does he put the workers under some sort of spell? Or can he punish them in ways that go beyond anything OSHA regulates?

The only thing that got RJ moving was the fear the witch might somehow trace him to his car. He checked his rearview mirror every few minutes, took a roundabout route with switchbacks on the way to his motel, and scanned the parking lot for threats before he dodged to his room.

When he got inside, RJ leaned with his back against the door, still freaked out. Once he caught his breath, he peeled off the warehouse clothing and poured himself a stiff drink. *What the ever lovin' fuck was that?*

He swore under his breath as he paced. *Shit, shit, shit. When did Osterman get a witch?*

Does that change my plan?

Depends on how powerful his witch is—and whether he's good at playing detective.

RJ sat and nursed his drink, deep in thought. If Osterman really did have a witch—instead of just a creepy sidekick who liked to glare at people—that was a level of security RJ hadn't factored into his plans.

Then again, he wasn't attacking the warehouse owner's physical safety—just his financial security and reputation. Maybe—hopefully—cause him some jail time. Would a witch care about that?

RJ drained his glass and filled it again, deciding that it didn't matter about magic—he intended to finish his mission for Mick's sake.

Once resolved, he turned on the burner phone connected to the security cameras and opened the file where the videos saved every few minutes.

Despite the size of the warehouse, the glaring fluorescent lights illuminated the space sufficiently for the cameras to pick up decent images. RJ watched for fifteen minutes and spotted a slew of violations, some minor and others major. He smiled, knowing the video would bolster his case, and set the phone aside.

RJ peeled off his clothes, too tired to shower. He stripped to his briefs, slipped under the covers, and fell asleep hoping that he would dream about Bart with a sexy and satisfying resolution.

RJ SPENT an hour during breakfast making calls and lining up appointments. Then he showered, made sure his hair looked good, checked the warehouse camera feed, put his suit on, and got down to business.

He knocked on the door of a small shotgun house that had seen better days. A grizzled man with tired eyes and salt-

and-pepper hair opened the door.

"Mr. Sawyer? I'm Keith Lang, the OSHA representative. We spoke on the phone."

"Yeah, I remember you. Don't know why you're talking to me now—you're about ten years too late," the man said. He wore a tank top that revealed ropy arms and stained jeans.

"It's never too late," RJ told him, sinking into his role.

Hammond indicated two rocking chairs on the porch. "Sit a spell. Tell me what's so gosh-darned important." He limped to the rocker closest to the door.

"We've had several recent reports about safety violations at Osterman's Freight." RJ peered through his tortoiseshell glasses and settled into the other rocker. The air smelled good here, clean, and it carried a trace of recently mowed grass.

Hammond snorted. "Ought to be several *hundred*. I don't know anyone who ever worked there who didn't get hurt some way. My leg got wrecked, but I'm one of the lucky ones. Folks lost fingers and hands, broke their backs. Died—or worse."

RJ raised an eyebrow. "That's exactly the sort of thing I need to document so we have a better chance of hitting Osterman where it hurts—in his wallet."

"You got that right." Hammond cackled. "And no one deserves it more. What do you want to know?"

"Let's start with the basics. Did you receive regular safety training?"

"Nope."

"Did that change over the years you worked there, for new hires and existing workers?"

"Nope."

"Were you issued protective gear—reflective vests, steel-toed boots, hard hats, gloves, that sort of thing?"

"Hell, no."

RJ took notes, but he also had his phone recording in his pocket. The answers didn't surprise him, but they suggested a much larger scope of damage to people's lives beyond his brother's death.

"Did workers petition for better conditions?"

Hammond gave him the side eye. "Do I look stupid to you? We could ask until we were blue in the face, for all it would change anything. If you wanted the job, needed the paycheck, you just kept working. Once in a while there'd be a young fool who didn't know better, or someone who just got fed up who tried to get something fixed. They didn't last long."

"Fired?"

"Mostly. I recall the cops being called out on one or two who made enough noise someone might start poking around. Sometimes bad things happened to 'troublemakers.'"

"Like what?" RJ pressed.

"Car accidents on lonely roads. Houses burned down. Bullet through their front window, rock through their windshield. People hereabouts might not have much schooling, but we're not dumb. We can read the writing on the wall." Hammond touched a finger to his nose.

The charges didn't surprise RJ, but he felt sick to his stomach hearing them confirmed. "Did OSHA inspectors ever tour the warehouse?"

Hammond sighed. "We saw guys like that once in a blue moon. Nothing ever came of it. We all figured Osterman paid them off to ignore anything they saw."

"If the warehouse had an unusual number of serious accidents, didn't the police or the hospital notice?"

"Son, I don't know where you're from, but in these parts a couple of things are true. First—everyone's related to everyone else. And second, we have the best cops and judges money can buy, owned lock, stock, and barrel by the people with the biggest houses in town. And guess who owns one of those big houses?"

RJ didn't have to guess. "Osterman."

"Figured you for a smart boy when I saw those glasses."

"I know you've been retired for a while, but if you remembered any of the accidents enough to give me names, details, and an approximate date, it would help document the case," RJ said.

Hammond glared at him. "You keep my name out of it, you hear?"

RJ crossed his heart. "I promise." If he had those details, public records should be enough to verify without dragging the old man into it.

Hammond leaned back in his rocker and didn't speak for a few moments, staring out at the woods across the lane. "First month I worked there, Kenny Richards lost two fingers in a conveyor belt. Couple of months after that, Darla Fanning got her leg crushed when a forklift rammed her into a stack of boxes."

Hammond reeled off incident after incident, fast enough that although RJ wrote as quickly as he could, he was glad for the recorder in his pocket.

If these are the ones that stuck in his mind because they were bad, there are probably hundreds more that weren't as dire. It's amazing the whole town isn't maimed.

"'Course, there were also the ones who died," Hammond said, losing his snark and sobering. "Happened way more than it should have. Hell, people shouldn't die trying to make a living. Pallets or boxes fell over, people driving the damn equipment didn't look where they were going, machinery threw a bolt. Lots of ways to die."

RJ already knew that Hammond hadn't worked for the warehouse when Mick was killed, but hearing the details about how many others died because of Osterman's negligence stoked RJ's fury.

"Are the rumors about shipping drugs true?"

Hammond hesitated. "We all believed them. I didn't see anything myself, but people I trusted said they did. Osterman didn't pass up anything that made him money, no matter who he had to deal with. I doubt drug dealers scared him. He had *protection*."

RJ hadn't been particularly impressed by the warehouse's security, so he filed the comment away and decided he'd come back to it.

When Hammond grew silent once more, RJ circled around to the question that stuck in his mind. "Early on, you said people died—or worse. What's worse than death?"

The old man seemed to weigh the likelihood of being believed and must have figured "what the hell." "Getting hexed, if you believe in that sort of thing—and anyone who crossed paths with Osterman's witch did."

"Hexed? Witch?" RJ's heart sped thinking of the round-faced man.

Hammond nodded. "I only ever heard him called Schultz. Don't know if that was his real name. Short guy with a big head and mean eyes. No idea where he came from or where Osterman found him."

"Was he there the whole time?"

"Nope. Showed up the year I got hurt. I wasn't happy about fucking up my leg and getting let go, but getting out from under that cockroach was almost worth it."

"How do you know he was a witch?" RJ doubted Hammond was psychic, although plenty of people had strong intuition without other abilities.

"Once he was around, weird things started to happen. People the supervisors didn't like would get a run of bad luck —everything from catching shingles to car trouble to having their garden rot. Only seemed to happen to the ones who caused trouble," Hammond replied.

"It was never like in the movies, with weird symbols or freaky dolls or that sort of thing," he went on. "Folks around here are church-going types. They might have caused an uproar if they found chicken bones or animal sacrifices. There was never any proof—but we knew anyhow. People had the local priest come out and bless the warehouse. Didn't do a lick of good, but soon after that the rectory got hit with lightning, and didn't that just prove the point?"

"Was there more besides the bad luck?" RJ knew that magic and paranormal abilities were real, and whatever Hammond had seen seemed to have gotten past the old man's skepticism.

Hammond's expression grew pensive. "You know most folks won't believe you—except the ones who know better and can't do squat about it."

"Gotta start somewhere," RJ replied with a wan smile.

"The bad luck could be real bad. Car wrecks, falling down stairs, freak accidents. Always happened soon after there'd been a problem with someone. One time, right before I left, I saw Schultz look right at a man and mutter something, and the fellow grabbed his chest and fell down dead on the spot. They said it was a heart attack, and maybe that was true, but God himself couldn't tell me Schultz didn't cause it." Hammond turned toward RJ with a fierce intensity in his watery blue eyes.

"Wow." RJ didn't have to fake his reaction. Hammond's terrifying story validated the vision he'd had and his impression from seeing the black clad witch.

"If you're going to write a report, better do it somewhere outside of Jackson," Hammond advised. "Osterman's got the town in his pocket. The ones who aren't on his payroll won't say 'boo' because of his witch. So you'd best go to Nashville,

Memphis, or Chattanooga, where people are too sophisticated to believe in hocus pocus."

RJ had grown up not far from here, so he knew small-town folks. Everything Hammond told him rang true.

"I know I've taken up a lot of your time, Mr. Hammond, and I'm grateful to you," RJ said. "Is there anything else before I go?"

Hammond fixed him with a stare. "That witch hexed a priest. Nothing scares that devil. If you're going to meddle in this, best you watch your back."

"I'll keep that in mind. Thanks again for your help." RJ's gift had been good at warning him in the past, and he hoped it would be enough.

He drove away, glimpsing Hammond still sitting on his porch. RJ believed the man's story, but he knew no one official would buy into the idea of witchcraft.

If Osterman was working with the Mafia or the cartels, that would make the evening news. It's not really funny, but the folks around here used to get their knickers in a twist about D&D and rock music being "of the devil." They saw Satan under every bed. Now they've got a real live dark witch playing havoc in their lives, and they don't know what evil actually is.

A frightening possibility occurred to RJ as he drove to his next appointment, another former warehouse worker who had agreed to help OSHA. *If I could pick up on a tingle of the witch's power, could he sense me? And what will I do if he comes after me?*

The next two interviewees echoed Hammond's stories of danger, drugs, negligence, and supreme disregard for worker safety. Just as importantly, they also told frightening stories about Osterman's witch and dire curses.

RJ drove back to the outskirts of Memphis, blaring his radio to keep his dark thoughts at bay. He needed time to digest what he'd heard and factor in this new potential obstacle to his plans.

At least the witch wasn't around when Mick died. Is it a good thing that magic wasn't involved, or even worse, that greed and awful working conditions were deadly on their own?

Everything he had learned just reinforced RJ's desire to bring Osterman to some sort of account and make him pay, even if he didn't serve time for his crimes.

BACK IN HIS ROOM, RJ ate dinner, turned on the television, and found a show about people looking for a house on the islands. He smiled, thinking about his dream of retiring to somewhere with a beach and palm trees—with Bart.

RJ palmed his crotch, pressing against his hard cock. He closed his eyes and slouched in his chair, spreading his legs, then unzipped and shoved his hand into his briefs, making his fantasy even more real.

He didn't just want Bart for a few hours or a night. He'd seen him sprawled on a king-sized bed, loose-limbed and hungry. Wanted to drink in those miles of tanned skin again and again. RJ wanted to know the scratch against his lips and cheek, the scent where Bart's musk was strongest.

Would he switch? They hadn't gotten that far yet, but it was clear they were both thinking about taking that next step. RJ preferred men who liked to trade places. While he often bottomed, he could enjoy topping as well. He imagined them together one way and another, both equally good. He thought about dragging his fingers down Bart's back in the midst of passion, or feeling his lover nip along his spine as he was being ridden from behind.

His imagination proved convincing enough to his body to

send him over the edge, and he stroked himself through climax, breathless and damp with sweat.

In his fantasy, when they'd both been satisfied, they stayed in bed together, blissed out and content. Safe with each other and from the outside world. He imagined conversation in the dark confessional of their bedroom, where neither of them had reason to hide.

He pictured spending the night tangled up with Bart in a room where they could hear the distant sound of the ocean, lit by the moonlight streaming in the window.

RJ imagined Bart's lightly calloused hand caressing his cheek, stroking his bare arm, pulling him close. He'd sink his fingers into Bart's dark mane of hair—longer since they left responsibilities behind—and pull him in for a kiss that was by turns claiming and gentle.

The mental image of them in the half-light and partial shadow of a moonlit room, naked but not revealed, turned him on just as much as seeing everything, especially when the faint glow caught a glimmer on their left hands. Married. Full partners.

He opened his eyes, and the bubble burst.

RJ roused out of his endorphin high as come cooled on his fingers, and his briefs felt sticky. He cleaned himself up with napkins and went to change clothing and wash up. The drop after the orgasm seemed more brutal than usual as RJ was alone in a darkened motel room with only the Travel Channel for company.

I picked this path. I could have figured out a way to live a more normal life—done things the official way, got a "real" job, found a partner. Kit and Mick wouldn't begrudge me happiness. They wouldn't have wanted me to spend my whole life bent on avenging them.

But if I don't avenge them, who will? Because it wasn't just them. *There are so many others who were hurt just as bad, and the system will never do right by them.*

Maybe I'll get away with everything and make it to a little beach somewhere. I might meet someone and be okay.

Or maybe it all goes wrong, and I get shot escaping. I die or I end up in Riverbend for the rest of my life.

I know which one is more likely, given the life I've led. And if it goes ass up, I'll have still done what I set out to do.

But I sure do like the idea of the Maldives a whole lot better.

CHAPTER FIVE

Bart

Four days into his new assignment, Bart couldn't help thinking that the Bureau had put the wrong agent on the job. Whetherby had been certain that Ghost Boy belonged on the Most Wanted list, and he'd done a good job of convincing Bart's boss as well.

But the more Bart reviewed his predecessor's notes and dug into the details, the less he trusted Whetherby's assessment.

The fraud itself wasn't in question. Everything else didn't make sense. Bart knew he could put his energy into following the path Whetherby had laid out, call in help from some ghosts, and probably crack the case, earning a commendation, maybe a raise. It wouldn't look bad the next time promotions came around, either.

Except...Bart couldn't shake the feeling that there was a much bigger game afoot.

Maybe the end would be the same no matter which path

he took, with Ghost Boy in prison and him on to his next assignment.

Or perhaps there were other possibilities, although right now Bart couldn't say what those might be. At the very least, it might be the difference between Ghost Boy getting a life sentence as a terrorist versus a dozen years, give or take, for fraud.

It shouldn't matter. I'm here to catch the bad guy, not psycho-analyze him.

But what if there really is more to this...

Bart plopped down on the couch and turned on the television while he ate lunch—an Italian hoagie and chips he had picked up when he left his suit and shirt off at the dry cleaners. A local news program came on, but Bart only halfway paid attention as he bit into his sandwich.

"I thought I could trust him because he talked like he was a person of faith," the aggrieved man told the reporter. "I trusted him to help stretch our cash to take care of the foster children, but the money's gone and so is he—and there's nothing in the new account like he promised. "Isaac Jamison is a fake, and I fell for it."

Bart's head snapped up at that last comment. *I, J. Holy shit —Ghost Boy strikes again.*

He noted the name of the victim—Joss Carmody. Bart's eyes narrowed as he thought. *It's been a while since I looked at anything to do with foster care, but I don't think they're supposed to go investing their stipend in dodgy get-rich-quick schemes. So on top of being out his cash, Carmody might be admitting to some fraud of his own.*

The interview cut away to the two immaculately dressed news anchors. "Although Mr. Carmody has reported an investment scheme gone wrong, an article in today's *Jackson Sun* alleging a history of child welfare issues—including neglect and physical abuse—has led to an investigation being opened against the Carmodys," the newscaster reported in the professionally serious tone of her trade.

"Looks like someone might have scammed a scammer," her co-anchor replied, and Bart bet the man had been captain of his football team in high school and was still chasing that faded glory. "Maybe we have a modern-day Robin Hood on the loose."

The newscast moved on to other topics. Bart clicked it off and stared at the darkened screen.

He opened his laptop and navigated to the newspaper website. It wasn't one of the big papers from Memphis or Nashville but a news outlet for a medium-sized town between the two cities. Big enough to have an internet presence with a much larger reach than its subscriber base.

As Bart poured over the well-written article, his mind raced with possibilities. The reporter, Jake Cooper, had done an excellent job and probably had a promising future with an award or two for investigative journalism.

Any sympathy Bart might have had for Carmody vanished as he dug into the meat of the article. Cooper laid out a wealth of evidence to show that the Carmodys had been bilking the foster system for more than a decade, taking money intended for their charges' care and withholding basic necessities. Some of their former wards spoke candidly to Cooper about beatings and hunger and living in fear of their caretakers' volatile moods.

Even worse, Cooper found information that suggested a few children had died under questionable circumstances while in the Carmodys' care, and others had run away with little to no effort made to find them.

Technically, fraud sometimes fell under the Bureau's purview, although perhaps not as often for the supernatural branch of the agency. Still, all of Bart's experience, and perhaps some of his magic, told him that this trail was important.

He sent in a records request for the names and disposition of all of the children who had been sent to the Carmodys over the past twenty years. That would take a while, even with computerized databases.

Next, Bart found an email address for the newspaper reporter and sent a polite request for an unofficial conversation about the article. He included his number, but didn't expect to hear back quickly, if at all.

In the meantime, he did a quick search on the reporter. Cooper had won multiple journalism awards for reporting on breakdowns in the local government and social service systems that put people at risk or took advantage of those without resources to defend themselves. He clearly wasn't afraid to speak the truth, and Bart wondered if the man had put himself in danger for going after people in positions of authority.

That just lent more credence to his exposé, which made Bart's thoughts whirl faster.

To his surprise, his phone rang minutes later.

"Agent Gibson? I'm Jake Cooper. I got your email. I don't know if I can help you, but I'll try."

Bart's strength was necromancy, but his magic also enhanced his intuition, and Cooper's voice held a sincerity that he liked right away.

"I read your piece—very well done. You'd have made a good detective."

"That's the 'investigative' part of reporting," Cooper replied. "On a good day, what I do makes a difference. I'm hoping this is a good day."

"Why did you write about the Carmodys? What sparked

you?" Truth spells were unethical and didn't work well over a distance, but Bart didn't need one to feel certain Cooper was telling what he knew.

"I have a soft spot for anything to do with kids," the reporter confessed. "This isn't my first piece bird-dogging people who take advantage of children they're supposed to be helping. Some of those pieces helped stop the abuse and drew attention to fixing holes in the system."

To Cooper's credit, he didn't sound like a crusader even though his passion shone in his voice. Bart understood the desire to make the world a better place. That desire had attracted him to study criminal law and apply for the Bureau, although a stint in the Army in between made him more jaded about the odds for good versus evil.

"How did you get a bead on the Carmodys?" Bart asked.

Cooper hesitated. "You know I won't reveal my sources, even if you subpoena me."

"I wouldn't expect you to."

"Although in this case, I couldn't anyhow. I met someone in a chat room, and we struck up some conversations about the foster system. They'd read my work; I was flattered. After we'd been talking for a few months, they offered me what they claimed was 'ironclad' research exposing Joss and Molly Carmody as abusive foster parents and outright criminals."

"They?"

Cooper chuckled. "The contact didn't give me a name, and the online handle was unisex. Which I won't share, but I'll tell you that I went back to check, and the accounts are all deactivated."

"Interesting." Bart frowned, thinking. "So you took the informant up on the offer?"

"Sure. I was wary. But everything checked out. Whoever set this up did the legwork. Names, dates, accounts. A clear paper trail that the money wasn't being used in approved ways and didn't benefit the children." Cooper's anger colored his tone. "I went to the mat to validate the intel, and it was all true. I guess no one ever cared enough to pay attention before this. There are problems throughout the foster system. That's not news. But this was a lot of evidence of long-time wrongdoing—and the guy had passed himself off as a youth pastor at one time, which is even worse."

Bart's guts twisted. In both the Army and the Bureau, he'd been part of sprawling systems founded on good intentions that often went awry due to incompetence, corruption, or just being too big to manage.

"I only caught part of the interview with Carmody. What's got him so riled?" Bart asked.

"Carmody and his wife are super religious. Or claim to be. That's gotten them the benefit of the doubt more than once when something questionable happened," Cooper replied. "And this time, it looks like the con man got conned. Some guy who claimed to be a 'Christian Investment Broker' offered him a sweetheart deal in cryptocurrency."

"Crypto?"

"Carmody clammed up on the details, but reading between the lines, I think this Jamison guy promised him amazing returns in a way that wouldn't be noticed by the IRS," Cooper went on. "The foster stipends don't count as income and aren't taxed, but they're not supposed to be used for investment, and any capital gains on an investment like that would be taxable."

"So Jamison skipped out with all their money?" That fit the "Robin Hood" angle but painted Jamison in a bad light. *I'm sure it's not his real name, but it's better than Ghost Boy.*

"Yes—and no," Cooper said. "He had Carmody write checks for an amount just shy of federal reporting regulations and go through all the paperwork as if he were actually buying crypto and hiding the gains. Jamison didn't cash the checks, then he tipped me off and sent everything, including the checks and account numbers to the IRS. He knew that once the article broke, there'd be hell to pay, the IRS would get shamed into investigating, and the kids would get moved. No kids, no new money. He didn't actually take any of Carmody's money, but all the steps to 'hide' it are incriminating as hell. If any of the oversight organizations do even a fraction of their job, the Carmodys will never get any more foster kids and will probably see some jail time."

"A highwayman with a heart of gold, huh."

"We all love to see someone who was above the law get their comeuppance," Cooper answered. "It's made for more than one bestselling book and blockbuster heist movie."

Bart heard the admiration in the reporter's voice and knew that Cooper wouldn't be cooperative in hunting down someone he clearly considered to be a champion of the oppressed.

He thanked Cooper and said that he might be back in touch but didn't get warm fuzzies about further contact being welcome. Bart couldn't blame the journalist for taking sides. Although Bart was sworn to uphold the law—and therefore the system behind it—he no longer held illusions about inerrancy or righteousness.

When it's not logical, it's personal.

Bart didn't need magic to have a gut feeling Jamison—or whatever his name was—had a dog in this hunt. Odds were good that either he'd been one of the Carmodys' foster kids or cared about someone who had been.

But what do skeevy foster parents have to do with a machinery company owner, a cop, and a guy who ran a Ponzi scheme? There's got to be a connection.

Whetherby hadn't looked to the perp's past to suss out a

motive, because he thought he had it all figured out. Now, Bart felt certain the other agent had been completely wrong.

It might not change the fact that laws were broken, but it's a hell of a different story trying to avenge wrongdoing than it is to be plotting some kind of terrorist attack.

Bart checked the time and realized it was early afternoon. He toyed with the idea of going to visit the Carmodys in an official capacity and figured that might strain his director's patience. He only had a hunch to connect their situation to his case, and he wasn't sure he'd find out anything more than the details Cooper already reported in his article.

Instead, he made a fresh pot of coffee and cracked his knuckles before turning on an old movie for background noise and getting down to business.

"I think I'm going to take another look at that machinery company owner, for starters," he muttered to the empty room.

Dennis Abbot was the CEO and co-founder of A&T Fasteners, a mid-sized company near I-40 just outside of Jackson. Bart couldn't imagine a more boring and mundane business. The plant made custom and special-purpose bolts, screws, and unusual connectors for companies across the Southeast.

Abbot had been the perfect small-town local success story, with a profitable company, pretty wife, well-behaved kids, and big house in a nice neighborhood. The company, which was founded in the mid-eighties, took off quickly. It had gone through a rough spot in the early 2000s but seemed to have pulled through.

Then two years ago, an anonymous tipster sent very detailed files to the FBI alleging that Abbot had committed white collar crime, including embezzling millions. The tip paid off, Abbot was convicted and did jail time, and the company was sold to a multinational corporation.

"Where's the supernatural angle? How did the TBSI get involved? I'm missing something." He spent an hour on each of the other cases—a crooked cop and a banker involved in a Ponzi scheme but came away equally unsatisfied.

"Fuck it." He picked up his phone, dialing a Nashville number.

Patrick Fergus, his research associate back at headquarters, picked up on the first ring. "Hey, Bart. How's it going? What can I do for you?"

Bart couldn't help smiling. Patrick always seemed game for whatever data dive Bart assigned him. *Nice to know someone who truly loves his job.*

"I got temporarily moved to Memphis, picking up on a string of cases for an agent who had a heart attack," Bart said.

"Yeah, I heard. Friday night darts and pool at the bar aren't the same without you. What do you need?"

"I'm looking at the files the previous agent put together, and I'm sure there's some important stuff missing," Bart replied.

"Are we talking witchy-ghosty stuff or regular stuff?"

"I've already spoken with the old agent's ghost. Let me tell you, he was a real piece of work. Which is part of the problem. I think he had his mind made up before he started investigating, and you know how that turns out."

"Usually puts you up shit creek without a paddle," Patrick agreed.

"I think I'm missing data—and the link to how these cases ended up with the Tennessee Bureau of Supernatural Investigation instead of the plain old feds. And all I can come up with is a suspicion that the person behind this is either a psychic or a witch."

"Okay. Talk to me. We'll figure it out, or I'll go dig up dirt." Patrick sounded eager.

Bart told him about Abbot's white-collar crime conviction. "Here's what I don't get—why did an anonymous someone go to so much trouble to document the crime and collect the evidence for plain-old embezzlement? The embezzlement alone didn't cost the workers their jobs or destroy an employer for the town. That kind of stuff usually gets pegged as a 'victimless crime.' So why did someone care so much?"

"Got a theory to point me in a direction?" Patrick asked.

"I think there was a victim we don't know about. All these cases feel like there was something personal behind the tipoffs," Bart confessed. "But what I've found online, and in the file, never went below the surface."

"Was the company privately owned? If so, there isn't quite as much documentation," Patrick mused. "Public companies have to declare everything out the wazoo. Maybe the connection goes farther back than the old agent bothered to look. I'll see what I can find. What's next?"

Bart shuffled the papers. "Mason Monroe got busted for a real estate Ponzi scheme. He sold investors into an upscale vacation resort on Lake Graham that was never built. The first investors made out like bandits, but the latecomers lost their shirts. Ghost Boy apparently tipped off the Federal Trade Commission with all the details, and the mastermind got sent to Riverbend." he said, naming the state prison.

"Ghost Boy?" Patrick laughed.

"Shut up," Bart said without heat. "That's what my boss calls him because so far, he's done all this without leaving a trace."

"So, not actually a ghost. I thought *Danny Phantom* might have gone dark side," Patrick joked. "Then where's the woo-woo?"

"Exactly. And how did the cases get lumped together?" Bart ran a hand through his hair and over his face. "I hate to speak ill of the dead, but Whetherby seemed to just accept face value and run with it. I think there's something a lot bigger that's the key to the whole damn thing."

"Okay—is that all?"

"Two more," Bart told him. "A banker. Same thing—a file fully documenting serious loan mismanagement, mortgage fraud, and illegal property seizures got turned in to the SEC. Someone convinced him to grant loans to a fake movie production company that ended up shooting pornos. He got off on jail time but paid a butt-load of fines and can't work in banking again."

He paused to swig more coffee. "And someone turned in evidence alleging gross misconduct about a cop and his supervisor from Medina to the state attorney general. Illegal arrest, failure to provide detainees with critical medical care, illegal search and seizure, possession of illegal drugs with intent to sell, and sexual harassment. Both the cop and his boss lost their jobs."

"That's a really strange collection of crimes," Patrick agreed.

"Another thing they all had in common—someone was leaking info to social media and reporters before the big reveal in every case," Bart said. "That ginned up public interest and put pressure on the oversight agencies to make an example of the cases."

"*Before* the reveal? So you think it was this Ghost Boy working PR as well as being the PI? Or something psychic?"

"I don't know enough to have more than a theory—which is why I need you to see what you can unearth."

"You're the necromancer," Patrick joked. "You usually handle what's dead and buried."

"Find me some dead people to talk to, and I'll do my thing," Bart responded. "Here's my kernel of a hypothesis. One guy is behind setting each of these men up for a fall and making sure the charges don't get swept under the rug. Probably someone who was originally local since none of the people who got in trouble were big fish except in their hometowns."

"But were they important enough locally that they got away with their crimes because officials looked the other way?" Patrick asked. "I'm betting when we find the connection it won't be recent. That gives me an idea of where to focus."

"Right now, we've got jack shit," Bart confessed. "Ghost Boy used a different name with every case, although he signed his work by using aliases that move down the letters of the alphabet. He didn't step up to collect any rewards or claim involvement. But I think he still wanted to leave his mark."

"Interesting. Off the top of my head, I'm betting this landed with TBSI because your perp is probably psychic," Patrick suggested. "Or some of the people he sent away were using magic or something supernatural to help hide their crimes. You know regular law enforcement is allergic to woo-woo. They're afraid of getting wackadoodle all over them."

Bart laughed. "Ain't that the truth." While TBI and TBSI were officially equal organizations, Bart had felt the sting of condescension and skepticism from his peers at the sister agency.

"All right, let me start digging. I'll keep you posted as I find stuff and send you copies. And if you want to bounce more ideas around, I'm your guy," Patrick told him as they ended the call.

Bart stretched, needing to get out of his apartment. He headed out with no particular place in mind, deciding to take advantage of the nice day to stretch his legs.

He tried to clear his mind, but with so many unanswered questions he couldn't stop thinking about the case.

Are any of Ghost Boy's aliases real? There's got to be a thread that connects everything—but how far in the past do we need to dig?

How did Ghost Boy learn how to set his targets up? Is he ex-CIA? Former law enforcement? A pissed-off lawyer? The social media component is genius. He knows that without pressure the powers-that-be will do nothing, especially if the target has money and clout. So if he can make his marks toxic, their defenders peel away, and at least some justice is served.

Bart stopped at a coffee shop and got a large latte, then decided to take a stroll in a nearby park. He thought about Jon and smiled.

No one had gotten under Bart's skin in years, not since Shawn. He had done a lot of dating before he met Shawn and they got serious. The two of them had four good years together, only to have their dreams cut short. Bart had sworn he wouldn't get involved again, wouldn't risk his heart—and he hadn't.

But if anyone could make him change his mind, it might be Jon.

Yes, there was plenty of chemistry, and the sex so far had been fantastic, if rushed. Bart sincerely hoped that they had the chance to take things further, both as friends and in the bedroom, and see where this could lead.

Something about Jon "clicked" with Bart. He suspected that the other man had a touch of some sort of supernatural ability. Shawn had fully believed in Bart's talent as a witch and a necromancer, even though he had no magic of his own. At the time, that difference didn't bother Bart. So far Bart hadn't revealed that part of himself to Jon, but he had the feeling Jon wouldn't freak out.

He wondered what it would be like to have a partner who understood the "woo-woo," as Patrick called it. Magic and psychic ability could deepen a relationship, enhance sex, bind partners closer together. Bart had considered those things for after he and Shawn got married. He wondered how Shawn would have taken the suggestion.

Bart walked slowly around the small pond and watched the ducks. When Shawn died, Bart had been certain that the memories would never fade, that the sight, sound, and scent of his lover were etched so deep in his bones that he couldn't forget. And for a while, that was unbearably true. Every little thing reminded him of Shawn, making the ache in his heart so acute that sometimes Bart wished the accident had taken them both.

Maybe it was getting the closure of seeing Shawn's killer brought to justice, or just the passage of time. But now and then, Bart would be seized with remorse when he couldn't quite remember how Shawn sounded singing along with the radio or what his favorite takeout meal had been at a particular restaurant.

Bart, more than most people, knew that Shawn had moved on and wouldn't feel slighted. He'd seen his partner's soul depart for whatever came next, a better place. But when those moments happened, Bart still felt overcome with the feeling that he had let Shawn down by not holding fast enough to his memory.

It had taken Bart two years before he could even think of dating. His schedule as a TBSI agent kept him busy enough to be distracted and gave him few evenings at loose ends. Worse, he could get called out at any time, making it hard to guarantee that he wouldn't have to cancel a date at the last minute. Not to mention how much Bart hated navigating the uncomfortable dance of dating or hooking up.

And then there was the fact that even in Tennessee's biggest cities, acceptance for LGBTQ individuals was tenuous and highly dependent on the situation. His supervisor and closest colleagues knew, but otherwise Bart kept his private life quiet. Nashville and Memphis offered some clubs and bars, but he locked that side of himself down tight when he worked a case in small towns and rural areas.

Before he met Jon, Bart had only managed a few rushed encounters, all of which left him feeling lonelier than before. Relocating to Memphis away from his colleagues made that worse. He didn't know what led him to Haggerty's that first night. But approaching Jon had felt natural, and even without a lot of conversation they seemed to click.

Now that they had spent more time together, Bart remained intrigued. He didn't know what Jon usually did for a living, but given his own restrictions, he hadn't pushed to learn about the other man's background just yet. They had plenty in common as it was with movies, books, and bands.

He liked that Jon seemed willing to let their friendship move at its own pace without rushing things. *Maybe we'll just be fuck buddies for a while. That wouldn't be terrible, but there's something about him that I think I could really like. It's dangerous feeling like that, but I think I might be ready to take a risk.*

It would be nice to have someone of my own. Bart knew from watching the people he worked with that those who didn't have a life partner or close family tended to get worn thin by the job. Seeing the ugly side of the world was hard enough even with good coworkers and supportive bosses, but without more to life than work, he'd seen agents spiral into dark places.

I don't even know if Jon lives in Memphis, or if he's also just in the city temporarily, but if he's from around here we could still see each other when I go back to Nashville. Find out where things lead. I have a feeling that we could be good together.

He took another swallow of his now-cool coffee and chucked the empty cup into a nearby trash can. One of the ducks on the bank turned to look at him as if he had disturbed the peace.

His thoughts wandered back to the Carmody case. Bart's own upbringing had been well-off, the son of a prominent lawyer father and a socialite mother. He'd never lacked for anything—except the attention of his parents, who were too busy being connected and fabulous to stay home, and never seemed to quite know what to do with Bart once they had him.

Nannies and servants meant he never went unsupervised, hungry, or without comforts. As an only child, Bart loved playing video games, watching crime dramas, and reading mysteries...all of which played a role in his choice of college major and profession.

But for all his family's affluence, Bart never remembered his parents seeming particularly happy, and he hadn't been surprised when they divorced when he was in high school. He stayed with his father in Nashville while his mother went home to Savannah, and as his father threw himself into his work to get over the split, Bart was on his own more than ever those few years before college.

I've got no room to complain, not when there are kids out there in foster care and worse situations. And especially not when they ended up with guys like Joss Carmody instead of someone who gave a damn.

He headed back toward the motel, stopping to look at a community board covered with posters for local events. He scanned the notices for open mic nights, comedy clubs, local bands, and nearby festivals. One in particular caught his eye.

"Come to the Carnival of Mysteries. Thrill to sights and sounds that will amaze and confound you," the broadside read. It looked like the ads for Halloween haunted houses, sensational enough to be titillating but not actually terrifying.

Since he could see and communicate with actual ghosts, fake haunts didn't impress Bart. Worse, most of the depictions of witches were downright insulting, especially when there was religious prejudice mixed in. And since his magic and training made him quite able to take care of himself, Bart didn't get the thrill of danger or the rush of adrenaline that seemed to attract regular people to those events.

Still, the Carnival of Mysteries seemed like a spooky-themed fair, something Bart hadn't encountered before. He noted the location and the performance dates. *I doubt I'll have the time, but the director did encourage me to see some of the local sights while I'm in town. Maybe I'll check it out.*

By the time Bart returned to his apartment, he found several emails in his inbox. One of them was the file he'd requested on the Carmodys. He moved his laptop from the table and got comfortable on the couch, then opened up the document and scrolled down to the earliest dates.

Whoever Ghost Boy is, he's old enough to know how to research, infiltrate, and document crimes, plus he's savvy about using social media to win support. And he's had time to plan his revenge, so this isn't a spur-of-the-moment thing. He's been thinking about doing this for a while, probably stockpiling resources, gaining skills.

Cooper said that the man who clued him about the Carmodys built a relationship first, gaining his trust, proving his own credibility. That's pretty sophisticated. So I'm going to bet that our whistleblower is at least late twenties to early thirties.

If he had ever been one of the Carmodys' wards, it must have been early in their stint as foster parents. That still left a few dozen possibilities. Bart stared at the screen and tried to think like a profiler.

He's smart, driven, focused, and resourceful, with a strong moral code and a sense of honor. He's also deliberate and pretty restrained, given the situation. I don't know what his connection is to the other people he's taken down, but if he or someone he loved ended up with the Carmodys, it's impressive that he went for public shaming and official punishment instead of bodily harm.

Bart never had reason to pay much attention to the foster care system, but now that he had the documents for just one set of caregivers in front of him, he felt appalled and sick that so many kids ended up with nowhere else to go.

That's not true. Some of the unwanted kids run away and end up on the streets or dead. Others get trafficked. The adults and the system fail them at every turn.

At first glance, none of the names stood out. With nothing more to go on than intuition, Bart didn't know how he could pick out one child from so many and guess Ghost Boy's identity—assuming he was among the wards listed.

He scrolled back to the earliest cases. They would be the right age now, at least, to fit his profile. Bart figured he would run the names through the system and see if he could rule anyone out or in.

A trio of names made him stop scrolling. Two boys and a girl, siblings. At least they'd been placed together, even if it was with horrible fosters like the Carmodys. He added them to his list, then found a couple more individuals who might be promising.

"Good enough for a first pass," he muttered. "If none of them pan out, I'll come up with a second batch."

Bart emailed his short list back to the person who had sent the file, asking for a records check. While he waited for a response, he decided to research where Ghost Boy's other targets had ended up, thinking that a visit or summoning their spirits might move the case along.

The machinery company owner was serving time at a minimum-security facility near Tipton, not too far of a drive if Bart chose to interview him. The banker was under house arrest, and the cop had died in a DUI, while the Ponzi schemer was in the state penitentiary.

Bart weighed his next possible moves. If the cop's ghost hadn't moved on, he could probably summon it, maybe get some information. But until he could narrow down the prospects, even the officer might not know which of his assault victims had destroyed his career. Bart didn't plan to do anything until he heard back from Patrick, but he knew he needed to come up with a plan.

His best access would be to Abbot, the former company president, and the Ponzi guy. Getting clearance to speak to them in jail wouldn't be difficult. The banker was no doubt lawyered up and had nothing to gain by attracting new attention.

Bart hated going inside a prison, not just for the claustrophobia or the generally oppressive nature of the places. As a necromancer, he sensed the ghosts that lingered in every jail, lost, damaged, angry, afraid to move on. He'd never been to a correctional facility that wasn't haunted. Some even had a priest do periodic blessings, but that wouldn't remove the ghosts or the shadow that dozens of restless spirits left on a place.

Tennessee tended to be a very conservative state with a lot of religious folks who wouldn't take kindly to the idea of a banishment ritual or some witchy protections, so Bart kept his peace and didn't offer to help.

Bart's gut told him to wait for details on the foster kids before making his next move. Once he had one or two possibilities, he could cross-check more easily against the other targets and narrow down the possibilities. It was likely that given the targets' long history of corruption, they had too many victims to recall who might have come after them.

Whetherby concocted a theory that made Ghost Boy into a monster. Maybe he was angling for a commendation or a raise for saving the world. Setting that aside, what charges are likely to stick?

Impersonating an unregistered financial specialist could be considered a felony. We don't have proof that he hacked into databases or broke into offices to obtain information. No one's been able to find a trail with real or fake credit cards, and it's not illegal to spend cash.

If he's so committed to staying under the radar, maybe he skipped paying taxes. That was enough to put away Al Capone. Or maybe he's got a secret identity and he only does this vigilante stuff in his spare time, like a low-rent Batman. Identity theft is a possibility, and while illegal, that's hardly on the scale of what Whetherby had in mind.

We don't have any evidence of him making threats or causing physical harm. No proven stalking, breaking and entering, or wiretapping. Parking tickets? That doesn't exactly qualify for a manhunt.

And he's brought the hammer down on four people who were overdue for comeuppance. He did our job better than we did—that might be the unforgivable sin. I've seen people plea bargain away much more serious charges in exchange for cooperation to help catch the bad guys.

Ghost Boy exposed the flaws in the system. We don't always try hard enough to get the real villains. There are going to be some folks that rankles, hurts their pride. They could call it "vigilante justice," even though he let the authorities make the bust. It's a dirty secret, but sometimes the folks in charge are petty enough to destroy someone just to remind them of their place.

Bart realized that he had begun to cheer for Ghost Boy once he found traction for his theory of overdue vengeance. He'd seen people who had done far worse than anything uncovered so far skate free because they were valuable to a high-profile investigation.

He did our work for us, and while the media helped turn up the pressure, none of these are going to be national news that nets a promotion for the director and glory for TBSI.

Ghost Boy is likely to get screwed over for doing the admirable thing, even if it isn't exactly the right thing.

Bart realized that at some point, he might have to make a difficult decision between doing his job to its fullest extent or serving the spirit of the law.

Depending on what he chose, it might cost him his badge.

CHAPTER SIX

RJ

*R*J hit send and watched the files upload, scarcely daring to breathe until he saw the two emails go through. One went to the DEA and the TBSI with the details of Osterman's operation and his witch, the other to Palmer for his exposé.

He thought about the phone number he had entered into one of his burner phones, the one Bart had slipped into his pocket. *I wish I could call him and celebrate together.*

He sat back and tried to make sense of the tangle of emotions that struggled to drown him. Satisfaction, because he had finished what he'd set out to do, gotten a measure of justice against the people who had destroyed his family.

Sadness, because it meant leaving Memphis—and Bart. Even though RJ had been meticulous in covering his tracks, there was still a chance that he had missed something and that sort of thing was likely to bite him in the ass if he was still anywhere in Tennessee. He had enough socked away in hard-to-trace accounts to live comfortably until he decided how he intended to reinvent himself.

I can stay a few more days, have that dinner with Bart. I have to see him one more time.

When he vanished, he wondered how hard the Bureau would try to track him. He expected that a warrant might be issued if they ever figured out his identity, but if not, in the absence of evidence and the fact that he'd done some of their work for them, maybe in time they'd forget all about him.

RJ hoped so, because Key West was a lot closer than the Maldives.

Speaking of which...I wonder if anyone's been hired to take over for Agent Whetherby and dog my heels.

RJ had figured out ways to keep an eye on the TBSI by monitoring newsfeeds and some less public forums. Which is how he found the name "Bartlett Gibson," and the news that Gibson had been transferred on temporary special assignment from Nashville to Memphis.

Now that he had a name, RJ couldn't resist digging deeper. He turned up several mentions, including commendations and mentions of Gibson's involvement with several Bureau-connected community service efforts.

Sounds like a fucking Boy Scout, RJ thought, already figuring how to adjust his false trail of hints and breadcrumbs to appeal to the new agent's likely presuppositions. He followed the name to a career networking site and read his bio.

Criminal justice major at Vanderbilt. Pricey college—must come from money. Ex-Army. Commendations and medals. Real straight-arrow sort. Dudley Do-Right.

Then a photo popped up, and RJ caught his breath. His heart thudded, and his mouth fell open in a gasp.

That's Bart.

Holy hell. The agent assigned to bring me in is the best lover I've had in years.

Guess that explains the high-and-tight haircut.

The revelation shook RJ much more than he expected. He worried that their encounters had been a honey trap, that the new agent had somehow known that RJ was gay and laid a snare for him.

But RJ wasn't a regular at Haggerty's, didn't let himself become a regular anywhere, so no one should have been able to predict that he'd be there that night or at the coffee shop. Not to mention that he was almost certain that neither his photo nor his fingerprints were in any law enforcement system.

Even more persuasive was how his psychic vibe had felt safe with Bart, almost contented. RJ couldn't read minds, but his ability to sense whether a person's intentions were good or harmful had saved his ass many times. Bart made him feel protected, cared for in a way he hadn't realized, which filled a deep hunger until their coupling stirred his emotions.

Maybe running into each other really was a weird coincidence. Or else he's psychic, like me, and saw right through me from the beginning.

He stared at the handsome man on the screen, looking professional in his suit and tie. *I know what his face looks like when he comes. I've heard the way his voice rumbles when he's hard as steel, how his hand feels on my cock.*

This is all kinds of fucked up. I'm fantasizing about bending him over a table and fucking him 'til his knees buckle—or vice versa—and he wants to put my ass in prison.

I think that counts as "irreconcilable differences."

Even if he wasn't the guy assigned to bring me in, even if I wasn't on the wrong side of the law, there's no way a guy like that would want more from someone like me than a quick fuck.

He's got looks, money, a career, and a badge.

My life's been a dumpster fire since I was five. Orphan, foster kid, runaway, thief, carny. Vigilante. Criminal.

Doesn't matter if we have enough fucking chemistry to set the world on fire. Nothing can ever come of it. Can it?

RJ had the advantage in that he knew who Bart was, but figured Bart had no idea that the man he'd fucked in a motel room and a barroom stall was on his Most Wanted list.

Would a police sketch be close enough, even with the changes I made, for Bart to recognize I was his hookup?

RJ poured a drink. He felt shaken, angry, hurt, and lost. Even so, he wasn't quite ready to let Bart go, although he knew they were doomed.

Is there any scenario in which I get to keep him?

First, I'd have to get past his over-developed sense of responsibility. Get him to see me as Robin Hood instead of Public Enemy Number One. Maybe give him my hard luck story to appeal to his need for justice and point out how I'm just putting right what the system didn't do.

Yeah, that might work. Play on his sympathy—not pity. He might have a fancy degree, but I'm smart too. Hell, all the online courses I've taken earned me a diploma. So we'd have to be equals. Maybe he saves my neck from the noose, and I watch his back, since a job like that makes enemies.

There are two ways this could go. He could make an honest man out of me. Maybe we'd start a private security company or be high-class bodyguards for billionaires. I think I read a book like that; only the characters spent more time getting blowjobs than dodging bullets. Which is nice work if you can get it.

We fuck like bunnies, he leads me to the light, I don't go to jail because I've done a public service stopping bad guys, and we buy a little pastel house in the Caribbean or maybe Key West. Wouldn't have to hide because we'd be legitimate good guys, only we'd make our own rules. And then when we got tired of going on adventures, we'd cash in and open a beach bar, maybe buy a boat and take tourists around.

RJ topped off his drink, needing a buzz. He reconsidered the direction his fantasy had taken.

I might be a lost cause for that. Maybe I could bring him to the dark side. We'd right wrongs for the little guy, but we'd have our own code. Plenty of last-day-on-Earth sex. Everything would be hot and desperate because we might die at any moment.

RJ savored the pictures his imagination conjured up. He saw Bart and himself in a Caribbean hideaway, naked and sweaty, making love. After a near miss, sex would be hot and rough, proof of life. But in between jobs, they'd be slow and tender, mapping out each other's skin with fingertips and tongues, taking their time.

Only then did he realize that he was blinking back tears.

It's a pretty daydream, but it's never going to happen. He'll hate me when he eventually finds out. He'll think I knew all the time and strung him along, that it was all a lie to throw him off the trail. Even if he did care, this will kill those feelings. Probably make him more intent on putting me behind bars.

And the worst part? Everything I felt for him is true. And fuck it all; I think I fell in love with him.

Guess we won't have that next dinner date after all.

Even if Bart didn't know who RJ really was—yet—RJ couldn't carry on the façade. It wouldn't be fair to either of them. Bart was going to be hurt and angry enough without giving him more reasons to believe he'd been conned. Except for using his "Jon" alias, everything else about their interaction had been honest and heartfelt. He cared too much for Bart to lie to him.

Let it die pure.

RJ only had seconds of warning before the vision washed over him. The motel room faded, and RJ didn't recognize the location.

Pain raced through his body, making him writhe. He struggled for breath and felt life slipping away with consciousness. He heard a distraught voice nearby, but it was too muddled to identify. Hands gripped him in a futile attempt, but RJ knew he was dying. He didn't know how, where, or why, but the "when" seemed fairly certain.

His visions never predicted the far future. Some version of what he watched, horrified, would happen soon.

RJ clawed his way back, and the last dark remnants of his vision faded. He found himself on the floor beside the table and hauled himself onto his chair. His hands trembled, and he was breathing hard. Cold sweat beaded his back.

The visions have always come true.

Guess I'm not going to make it to Key West or the Maldives.

When RJ finally stopped shaking, he walked to the bathroom and splashed cold water on his face, slicking back his sweat-soaked hair. The man who stared back at him in the mirror looked desperate and freaked out.

Did I get shot resisting arrest? Knifed in a back alley?

The vision left the details hazy, other than the single terrifying omen of his death.

His stomach growled, apparently disinterested in his imminent demise.

If that's how things are going to play out, I'm going to grab myself a damn good dinner. Fuck cholesterol. I want a burger worthy of a last meal.

RJ didn't risk driving since he had been celebrating with bourbon. He wasn't drunk, but it would be a shame to come this far and get arrested for DUI.

He walked to the diner, ordered takeout, and headed back, being extra careful to watch for traffic.

The motel's neon sign flickered and glowed in the twilight. A stocky figure emerged from the shadows, and RJ wondered if being mugged for his dinner was going to seal his fate.

"I think you left something behind." The man's deep voice held a trace of a German accent. The stranger held a small object between his thumb and forefinger, and in the dim light, RJ could barely make out one of his surveillance cameras—the kind he'd planted at Osterman's Freight.

Holy hell. It's Shultz, the witch.

The man spoke a command in a language RJ didn't understand. Glowing dark violet tendrils spun from his outstretched hand, racing toward RJ before he could even think to run. They wound their way up his body—cold, slick, and stinking of rot.

"You'll be dead within a fortnight, perhaps sooner." The tendrils faded, sinking into RJ's skin. "Whatever you thought to gain, you will not live to enjoy."

"Osterman killed my brother." RJ fell back on bravado because he refused to show terror.

Shultz shrugged. "All men die—some sooner than others. You will join him soon. Your last days will not be pleasant. You may survive long enough to regret your vengeance."

RJ blinked, and the witch was gone.

He hurried to lock himself in his room. His hunger for the food in the bag dangling from his wrist was gone, turned to cold dread.

Other people might dismiss a witch's curse as theatrics, but RJ's psychic ability knew true power when he encountered it. He'd felt the same malicious energy that night at the warehouse when he planted the cameras.

Had Shultz spotted me then and taken his time to come kill me? Or did he just find the camera and use it to trace me? He had heard of magic that could read the history of an object by touch.

I was so careful not to leave fingerprints, and a fucking witch manages to trace me anyhow.

Guess I can stop worrying about going to jail.

RJ dropped his bag on the counter and sank to the floor, curling up in a ball with his knees to his chest and his head in his hands. He could already feel the supernatural malady in his blood. RJ felt certain that no matter what the symptoms became, no medicine could cure him.

Osterman must have really been pissed. If Shultz could make a worker fall over dead on the spot—quick and relatively painless— then he reserved the worst for me. Giving me a few weeks wasn't a kindness—it was torture.

I am royally fucked.

Despite everything, RJ wished he could turn to Bart for comfort. If his lover really did have a touch of ability like RJ's senses told him, perhaps his magic would ease RJ's passing. But asking for help was out of the question.

I need a plan. I can't stay here, and there's nowhere for me to go. But I've got to find a place to hide.

When he had fled the Carmodys as a child, RJ had run away with the circus. The poster about the Carnival of Mysteries came to mind. If the faire really did have people with supernatural talents, perhaps someone could at least give him respite in his last days. If not, RJ could probably talk his way into a place to hide so he didn't die alone.

He forced himself to eat the cold burger, hoping it didn't come back up. A computer search didn't reveal details about the carnival, but RJ remembered the information on the poster. He would find it.

When he felt sure he wasn't going to throw up, RJ poured himself another glass of bourbon and started to pack. The carnival would be busy at night, but in the morning, he could show up and apply for work as a roustabout, which might give him a place to stay and food to eat for as long as he needed.

It didn't take long to gather his things. That had never bothered RJ before because he thought of his mission like being a soldier, and warriors traveled light. Now, his meager belongings and rootlessness taunted him with everything he had missed out on.

Was it worth the price I've paid? He decided it was, seeing the people responsible for tearing his family apart finally called to account.

I didn't get the life I could have had. But they lost everything. It was a worthy sacrifice.

RJ wondered how the curse would progress. Right now he felt mostly okay once the nausea subsided. Subtle signs like a headache lingered in the background, along with the vague achiness that usually marked the onset of the flu.

If I can walk into the carnival and then I get sicker after they take me on, they'll give me a good death. Carnival folks take care of their own.

He fell asleep recalling his date with Bart, how good it had felt to be wrapped in his arms, how perfect they had been together. *As last memories go, it was a hell of a ride.*

Will Bart look for me when I disappear, if he finds out the truth, that I was the man he hunted? RJ wanted to think that Bart would still harbor some fondness for him. He hoped that Bart could forgive him or at least let him go without hatred. Thinking that the truth might destroy any happy memories of their brief time together made RJ even sadder.

If they never link me to the cases, Bart will think I abandoned him. I'll hurt him, and I think he's been hurt before. I should have never gotten involved with him, but I don't regret our time together. I'm not sorry for falling in love with him, and I'll go to my grave believing that he might have loved me, just a little.

CHAPTER SEVEN

Bart

*B*art rubbed his eyes and reached for his coffee, which was stone cold. The puzzle pieces were starting to fit, but some were still missing. He was close, but not quite to his goal.

Ghost Boy had earned Bart's grudging respect—he did thorough research, presented his arguments logically and coherently, and provided excellent supporting materials. *Hell, his files are better than ninety percent of the case docs I've read in the Bureau. And his fieldwork is spot on.*

I could argue that he's done our work for us with four cases that went overlooked. It would be a shame to catch him and send him to jail.

Could we offer him a plea deal? There are a lot of extenuating circumstances.

Bart began jotting down his thoughts, writing a proposal for Director Boward. Ghost Boy hadn't killed anyone, and while he might have committed identity theft and impersonation, it didn't appear that any assets had actually been stolen.

Ghost Boy had left it up to authorities to bring the culprits to justice instead of meting out his own. The involvement of the media forced the hand of the agencies responsible, but strategic leaks weren't unheard of when it came to prodding the powers that be to do the right thing.

Bart intended to spend part of today interviewing spirits to bolster Ghost Boy's case. He had gotten the results back on what happened to the short list of foster children, learning that several had died or disappeared. Bart expected their ghosts to corroborate his theory that the Carmodys got what they deserved.

The cop's ghost was a longshot, difficult to coax cooperation, but perhaps worth a try. Regular mediums couldn't compel spirits or control them like a necromancer could, which tended to intimidate stubborn revenants.

If he could prove that Ghost Boy had good cause for his vendetta and had kept to relatively insignificant lawbreaking, he might be able to sell the director on clemency.

Bart laid out his argument for making a deal. Then he checked his spelling, murmured a minor luck spell, and pressed "send."

Next, he pulled up the short list of foster children. Out of the ten he had asked about, four ran away while in the care of the Carmodys, three were confirmed dead after leaving their care, and the location of the other three were unknown.

Bart got out his bag with the summoning materials. He drew a warded circle on the floor, set up the candles, and pulled out the silver bowl. He didn't have anything that had belonged to the three dead children, so he relied on a mix of dried plants that had power to thin the Veil.

"Jennifer Williams, Alexis Brown, Stephanie Wilson...I

bid you welcome and ask you to talk with me. I promise you will be safe. Don't be afraid."

Bart was used to speaking with the ghosts of adults, but he rarely had reason to interview children's spirits. Just the thought made him sad. He wouldn't compel these ghosts to speak to him—although he had the power—but he hoped they would not be so faded or fearful that they did not answer.

One by one, the three girls' ghosts flickered into sight. From their files, he knew they were all under fifteen when they died. One drowned, another was in a car accident, while the third was hit while riding a bike.

"Thank you for answering." He hoped he didn't seem intimidating. Bart hadn't had a lot of experience around kids. "I'm sorry for bothering you. But it's very important for me to find out the truth about what Joss and Molly Carmody were like as foster parents. I need you to tell me the truth, even if it isn't nice."

"They were mean." The girl who looked the oldest, whom Bart guessed to be Jennifer, spoke first. "Mr. Joss hit us if we broke any rules—and there were rules about everything. Mrs. Molly didn't like us. She made us do chores even if we were real sick, and there was never enough food."

"The food was yucky," Stephanie, the youngest of the trio, said. "Plain noodles. Oatmeal. Dry bread and cheese. We were always hungry. Sometimes, the food made us throw up."

"They yelled a lot," Alexis, the third ghost added. "Sometimes they even made the boys cry. We tried to take care of each other, but it was hard. There were mice in the house and rats sometimes, and the roof leaked."

"Did they take you to the doctor for checkups or when you were sick?"

All three shook their heads. "Mrs. Molly said that she could doctor us just as well. She made us drink awful stuff. If we weren't half-dead, she didn't do anything at all," Jennifer told him.

"Did you have clothing and shoes that fit, and coats for the winter?"

"We weren't naked, but everything was ratty," Alexis said. "Like the stuff the thrift store has for a dollar 'cos no one wants it. We wore what we had until it couldn't be patched. If we ripped the cloth or grew too fast, Mrs. Molly screamed at us. The shoes never fit right, either."

Bart struggled to control his anger. He had looked up how much the state paid foster parents per month for each child. The sum was definitely enough to provide necessities that weren't bargain-basement trash.

"Did anyone from the County ever check on you?" Bart knew resources and staffing were low, but he felt sick thinking that other kids were suffering from neglect like this right now, in other foster families.

"Sometimes," Jennifer said. "If he knew they were coming we had to put on the best clothes we had, and Mrs. Molly threatened to hit us with a belt if we said anything bad about them." The other two ghosts nodded solemnly.

"I'm so sorry that happened to you," Bart said, hearing the catch in his voice as he tried to control his emotions. "If you want to pass on, I can help you."

The three girls looked at one another, and each one nodded. "We'd like to go home now, Mister," Alexis replied.

Bart managed a wobbly smile. "Go in peace, free from the cares of this world, and follow the light to a place of safety and healing," he said, investing his words with all his necromancy magic.

The images of the three girls glowed, and a light grew bright behind them until the images faded, and the room was empty once more.

Bart closed his eyes and took a few deep breaths, trying to

let go of the churning in his gut and the ache in his heart. When he regained composure, he jotted notes on the file, although he suspected that anyone involved in overseeing the girls' care had long since moved on or the statute of limitations had expired.

He wasn't quite up to searching for the runaways just yet, so he opened the cop's file and poured himself another cup of coffee.

Jeb Holt, the police officer whose misconduct had been documented by Ghost Boy, was forty-six. He had been a cop since his late twenties, and lost his job a year ago thanks to the files sent to the state Attorney General's office.

TBSI had obtained a copy, which went into painstaking detail with a list of false arrests, illegal search and seizure, intimidation, sexual abuse, and a penchant for beating prisoners. Prior complaints had been made through the years, but the charges always got dropped, witnesses recanted, victims disappeared, or lenient judges gave Holt an irresponsible amount of latitude.

A list of people was attached, who had either alleged mistreatment or whose families had raised concerns on their behalf. Bart compared the list to the names of the Carmody foster children.

Only one last name matched. Emily Sue Tucker, whose sister—now deceased—filed a complaint that Emily had been denied medical care after being arrested for public intoxication, and that the lack of care led to her death.

Tucker. Just like three of the kids the Carmodys fostered. Bart felt the thrill of the hunt, unraveling the mystery at the heart of the case, which he enjoyed far more than the nightmare of shootouts and car chases.

He weighed the idea of summoning Holt's ghost and decided against it, at least for now. He doubted death had improved the cop, who had been a terrible person while he was alive and probably felt no remorse, even now.

He's dead. I know where to find him.

Armed with the last name, Bart went back to the banker's file. Among the listed victims of accelerated fore-closure was Emily Sue Tucker, whose house had been seized for allegedly missing mortgage payments. Documentation included in the dossier sent to the SEC proved otherwise.

Bart's scribbled notes filled page after page of his tablet. He examined the folder for Dennis Abbot, the owner of the machinery company. Halfway down the first page, Bart's eyes widened.

"Holy shit."

A&T Fasteners was founded by Dennis Abbot and Preston Tucker in 1985, the file read. *Eight years later, Abbot invested in a real estate development project run by Mason Monroe, and after doubling his initial payment, recommended the investment to his partner.*

Preston Tucker made a large investment without knowing that Abbot had ended his involvement with Mason, the report's writer alleged. *Preston and the second-level investors lost everything when the projects were revealed to be a Ponzi scheme. Abbot conspired with the A&T Board of Directors to force out Tucker and take his role as CEO. The combination of financial hardship and losing his stake in the company he helped to found drove Preston Tucker to take his own life.*

Bart double-checked the dates. Preston Tucker's death and financial ruin came six months before the foreclosure on the Tucker home and a year before Emily Sue's disastrous arrest. The three Tucker kids had gone into the foster system a week after her death with a note in the file that: *No imme-diate relatives were able or willing to provide care.*

Bart's mind was still spinning as all the pieces fell into

place. *Ghost Boy has to be one of the Tucker kids. Now I've just got to figure out who. Or were they all working together?*

His phone pinged.

Boward: *Turn on the news.*

Bart clicked the remote, and the local news channel came up automatically. The crawl at the bottom of the screen read: "Local Warehouse owner arrested in DEA/OSHA bust."

"Herbert Osterman, owner of Osterman Freight, was arrested today on a wide range of charges that include wage theft, numerous serious and ongoing safety violations leading to the death and permanent injury of workers, and alleged drug smuggling.

"An unknown informant provided detailed information to authorities that led to the arrest and sent a copy of that information to journalist Simon Palmer, an investigative reporter with the *Commercial Appeal*, whose story on the allegations was published just hours after the arrest took place," the newscaster said, as B-roll footage of Osterman being led away in handcuffs played behind her.

"This is a breaking story, and we will keep you updated as more information becomes available," she added before Bart switched to a channel running old television shows.

"There's got to be a Tucker connection," Bart murmured. Clearly Boward had thought the Osterman case bore an uncanny similarity to the rest of Ghost Boy's targets.

Bart weighed his options. He could call Patrick and see what his research assistant could unearth. That would take hours, no matter how fast Patrick was at digging.

Or I can see if I can find any of the Tucker kids, who would all be around thirty by now.

Once again, Bart opened the foster care file, but this time he knew what he needed. Three Tucker children—Michael, Kathrine, and Richard. A note mentioned their preference to be called Mick, Kit, and RJ. An addendum provided a date of death for Mick and said that Kit and RJ had gone missing, "whereabouts unknown."

Bart refreshed the materials in his silver bowl, discarding the ashes and cleansing the vessel before he renewed the warding and readied his mind to speak to the dead.

"Mick Tucker. I mean you no harm. I want to make sure that the people who hurt your family are punished. But I'm missing information. Please, show yourself."

Bart waited, and after a moment wondered if the ghost would refuse to answer. Then the temperature dropped and he felt a breeze in the still air. The spirit of a young man took shape just a few feet outside the circle.

"Michael Tucker?"

"Mick."

"Mick—how did you die?" Summoning ghosts took a toll on Bart's energy, and this was the second working today. He already felt fatigued, which meant he needed to get to the point.

Mick looked to be about seventeen, raw boned and broad shouldered, a little shorter than Bart with short, straight blond hair. He seemed underfed for his age and height.

"I was sneaking out at night from the foster home they stuck us in when Mom died—to earn money. I told Kit and RJ that once I turned eighteen and had enough saved, I'd to get them out of that place, and we'd go off together. I only had six months to go before I was old enough to apply to take care of them if I had a job and a place to live. And then it fell apart."

"Tell me."

Mick's ghost shrugged, still a moody teen. "I worked the night shift at the freight warehouse."

"Osterman Freight?"

"Yeah. It was the first job that accepted me, and I was desperate. Figured out real fast that they cut corners on safety, and sometimes they cheated on the pay, but I needed a job. Then one night someone lost control of their forklift, and I was crushed against the pallets. I bled out before anyone could even call an ambulance. And that was that."

"Someone just made sure that Herbert Osterman got charged with a whole lot of serious crimes," Bart told him. "I suspect he'll lose the business and go to jail for a long time."

Mick nodded. "Good. Except there will always be other guys like him."

"One less, now," Bart countered. "What about your sister and brother?"

"I don't know," Mick replied, looking sad. "I could never contact them. I just sort of drifted until I heard your call."

"Why did you call your brother 'RJ'?" That detail had caught his attention.

Mick gave a wan smile. "Because he hated the name Richard. So we called him Ricky Jon. RJ for short."

Jon. Oh my god. Ghost Boy is Jon.

Bart felt cold all over, but not because of the ghost. Shock coursed through him, followed by a sharp spike of betrayal.

"Is Jon—RJ—a redhead?" He realized he was holding his breath.

"Oh, yeah. Our ginger," Mick said with affection.

Bart could barely breathe, overwhelmed. "Do you have an idea of where RJ and Kit might have gone when they ran away after you died?"

Mick looked stricken. "They did? How long ago?"

"It's been about fifteen years, give or take," Bart told him. Time meant nothing to ghosts. Not enough had changed in the world for a spirit as new as Mick to easily see how long he had been dead.

"Kit probably ran to Nashville. She wanted to be a singer."

"What about RJ?"

Mick's expression darkened. "Why do you want to know?

You aren't going to make him go back, are you? I won't help you hurt him. I'll find a way to haunt you if you do." Mick's ghost seemed to gather energy as angry as his ominous expression.

"He's in trouble," Bart said, which was true. He felt heart-broken, used, and deceived, but knowing why Jon—RJ—had done what he did, Bart couldn't hate him for it.

"I care about him," Bart went on. *Also true. I've fallen in love with the bastard, and now where does that leave me?* "I need to find him before things get worse. I might be the only one who can help him."

Mick glared, mistrust clear in his face. He remained silent, and then relented. "RJ always said he wanted to run away with the circus. So maybe he really did."

"Thank you." Bart needed time to sort through his tangled emotions and responsibilities. "I can help you cross over, if you'd like."

Mick shook his head. "Not yet. Not until Kit and RJ are ready too. We should go together."

"Then depart in peace," Bart said, and sent a bit of his magic with his benediction. "I hope you find your family when the time is right."

Mick's ghost faded and disappeared. Bart stared at the empty room for several minutes, too overwhelmed to grasp the full impact of what he had learned.

Was it all a game to Jon? Despite now knowing his full name, Bart couldn't stop thinking of him as Jon. *Did he somehow know I was assigned to his case? Did he seduce me to discredit the investigation?*

But that really wasn't possible, Bart realized after he spiked his coffee with a liberal dollop of bourbon and sat down. *I hadn't started on the case when I met him at Haggarty's. TBSI hadn't announced my assignment. And I'm pretty sure that I did the seducing that first night.*

Bart searched for any way Jon might have figured out that he was tracking the Ghost Boy cases, and couldn't find a link. They had never talked about their jobs or personal history, keeping the conversation light and avoiding personal topics aside from superficial likes and dislikes.

If he somehow got a look in my wallet and found my official ID, then he's one hell of a pickpocket. Which I guess is possible, but even the night we slept together, I don't think he ever had the chance.

We slept together. I had sex with the guy I'm supposed to arrest. My career is toast.

Bart loved his job and had worked hard to climb the ladder inside the Bureau. He was proud of the work they did and the cases he'd helped solve.

Jon just solved five cold cases that we didn't even know existed. Is he going to jail for that?

It felt like his head might explode and his heart had torn in two.

If he forced himself into cold logic mode, he still believed that Jon's "vengeance tour" was deserved, even if he'd done the right thing in the wrong way. He admired Jon's tenacity, his skill in tracking down evidence, and his brilliant plan to prod both the media and the authorities to do their jobs.

From a purely logical standpoint, Jon deserved a reprieve, a chance to expunge his transgressions, and a way to start over—like the proposal Bart had pitched to Boward on Ghost Boy's behalf.

But his heart wasn't persuaded by logic. Bart had been surprised by how much he'd fallen for Jon, and how fast. After Shawn's death, he thought he would never love again. Then he met Jon, and in such a short time, everything turned around.

Bart had begun to think about a future where he wasn't

alone. About the possibility that maybe he could find a partnership in life and work. That a new start was possible.

Now...he didn't know what to make out of the tangle of emotions warring in his heart. He felt deceived—but Jon had given him his real name, if only part of it. Bart had never shared his last name or asked for Jon's, or mentioned his job. Funny that sex didn't require as much trust as sharing those details.

Sex...that hadn't been fake. He felt sure that he had seen real affection in Jon's eyes, felt it in his touch. He had been surprised at the depth of feeling their coupling had nurtured in him, something that hadn't been present in his few brief encounters since Shawn. To be honest, he'd never felt that kind of connection except with Shawn, and didn't think he would again.

He wasn't sure what stoked the white-hot surge of anger that he wrestled to control. Some part of him felt betrayed, lied to, used. That hind-brain fragment of himself wasn't listening to logic. It grieved, ranted, and stormed, whipsawing through Bart's heart.

Another part of his brain still wanted the man he had fallen in love with.

Even if we can't get past this as lovers, I don't want him to go to jail. He did what needed to be done, what the system failed to do. That shouldn't be a crime.

The television droned on, running a marathon of classic shows. Needing a break, Bart found himself intrigued by a show about a cat burglar who was offered a deal to stay out of prison as long as he agreed to work for the government, stealing things they wanted stolen.

That's it, Bart thought, eyes going wide. *That's how to keep Jon out of jail. Maybe we could be assigned to be partners. With his skills at putting together a sting—and some psychic mojo of his own —he'd be a natural.*

He wrote a follow-up email to Boward, this time suggesting that the deal include working with the Bureau as an intelligence analyst and offering to partner with "Ghost Boy." *In for a penny, in for a pound.*

An hour later, his phone rang.

"How's it going?" Boward asked. Bart was surprised it had taken six whole days on the job before the director started asking questions.

"Whetherby was wrong." Bart figured he would start as he meant to go on.

"Nothing like cutting to the chase," Boward replied with a chuckle. "I read your report—and saw your emails—but I'd like to hear it straight from you."

Bart laid out his reasons for disagreeing with Whetherby's hasty conclusions, the other agent's lack of thorough research or consideration of alternative theories, his interviews with his predecessor's ghost, and what he had gleaned from a fresh look at the data.

Boward was quiet for a moment when Bart finished. "Can't say I'm surprised," he said finally. "Hank was a good agent—on certain kinds of cases. He was close to retirement, and I think he got bitter and jaded. Hank didn't have a lot of patience or nuance, tended to see things in broad strokes. Good job on the analysis."

"Thank you, sir." Bart reminded himself to breathe. "What did you think of my proposal?"

"Very creative. Been watching late-night TV? My mother was a fan of Robert Wagner in *It Takes a Thief.* Your approach bears a certain resemblance." Boward sounded amused.

"Doesn't make it a bad idea," Bart countered. "I'm impressed by the legwork this guy has done, and how he managed to force closure on five cases that the authorities either ignored or mishandled. I'm pretty sure that he's a psychic—probably untrained—in order to do what he did.

And he writes up good case notes. We could use a guy like that."

"It would be unusual, but not unheard of. That show played fast and loose with some of the details, but it was based on real situations," Boward said, and Bart's hopes rose realizing that his boss was actually considering his proposal.

"So it's possible?"

"Theoretically. We'd need to get approval to offer him a deal, and before that we'd actually have to know his name and have him in custody, but considering the case you've made, and the lack of truly serious charges against him, I think we stand a good chance," Boward told him.

Bart grinned. "Good to hear, sir."

"Now you just have to catch the son of a bitch and find out his name. Are you any closer?"

"Fitting pieces together," Bart replied. He didn't want to give away too much before he could ensure Jon's safety.

"Good work. Keep me posted. There's a reason you came so highly recommended." Boward ended the call, and Bart couldn't resist a fist pump of triumph.

Could we really fix this?

What if Boward gets the proposal appeal to go through? Could we get past this to at least work together?

But Bart didn't want to just work with Jon. Trying to put the genie back in the bottle and have a platonic relationship would be hell. Bart felt too much attraction to Jon to just be friends. They had been too good together, even for a brief while, and he couldn't imagine that flame being extinguished.

Could we be lovers again? Is it possible to come back from this and create a relationship, or am I crazy to even want him?

It's only been three days since I've seen him. We're supposed to have dinner tomorrow night. I don't have his number, so I couldn't cancel even if I wanted to. Do I want to cancel? God, I don't know.

Maybe by tomorrow I'll have heard more from Boward about the proposal. I'd be on firmer ground, ethically, going through with meeting him with a deal in hand.

Technically, I don't have a confession or evidence, just suspicions. Eating dinner with an informant isn't a crime. Although having sex is definitely crossing the line.

I could be written up over this, lose my badge, become a laughingstock for having been played like a fool.

But, God help me, I care about him. I'm not ready to give up.

So I'll meet him for dinner, tell him about the deal, let him know that I found out about him. He'll either go for it or bolt, and I'll have my answer.

THE NEXT DAY seemed to pass slowly as Bart counted down the hours until his dinner "date" with Jon. He studied everything in the files, trying to connect the dots.

He tried calling for Kit's ghost, wondering if she had also died. No spirit answered. That might mean she was alive, or that her ghost had moved on already and was beyond his reach. Bart had no proof, but in his heart he believed she was dead, although he hoped he was wrong.

Richard Jon Tucker had no prior arrests, no fingerprints on file, and no photos. He also had no tax record, no driver's license, and beyond a birth certificate his official record ended when he ran away from the Carmodys.

He really is Ghost Boy. Even WITSEC couldn't hide someone this deep.

He's got to have a different identity that's good enough to hold up under scrutiny. No one manages to stay off the grid this well for so long.

Jon certainly hadn't looked homeless or penniless. He had

some sort of income to survive all these years. Now Bart wished he had paid attention to Jon's car or gotten his license plate number, but that hadn't seemed important at the time, and he had remembered Shawn's chiding not to treat everyone like a suspect, so he hadn't pried.

Bart found a death certificate for Emily Sue and Mick, but he could only locate a burial site for Jon's mother, in a plot beside his unlucky father. *Did the Carmodys deny Mick a decent burial? No wonder Jon had an axe to grind.*

The people Jon turned in to the authorities were all rotten. How many more victims are out there who deserved justice? Jon documented a lot of them, but odds are good he didn't know about them all. Were other lives ruined as badly?

Bart had started to put together a narrative about how it might have been for Jon. He wasn't naïve about what happened to young runaways or how much the odds were stacked against them just to survive and avoid being trafficked, or falling into substance abuse. He sincerely hoped Jon had avoided the worst of it.

He probably got jobs that paid under the table at first, because he wasn't old enough to work legally. If he created another identity, I don't know how to find a link. That would explain why RJ doesn't show up, although fingerprints would be a match. He might have a whole history out there, and I have no idea how to find it.

I can't believe I didn't even get his last name. Then again, he might not have told me the truth.

Once again, Bart was back to feeling hurt and betrayed. *I've got to get a grip before I see him at dinner tonight. This is all going to go to hell if I fuck it up.*

Will he even show?

Maybe he'll just leave town if he's finished getting revenge.

Is there anyone left on his list?

Despite everything, it hurt to think that he might never see Jon again.

Has he figured out who I am? He'd be a fool to keep the date if he has, because I'm a danger to him. If he has known who I was all this time, will he show up anyhow in some twisted celebration for putting one over on me? That was the bleakest possibility. Bart knew it would take a very long time to get over that level of betrayal. Maybe never.

He has my phone number.

Maybe I should not show up. No one else knows we had a date. It's my "get out of jail free card" for him. He could leave town, and we'll probably never find him.

But what if the deal from Boward comes through? What if Jon wasn't playing me? Suppose we actually could salvage this and make it work?

Jesus, I still want him.

Bart kept himself busy as the hours crawled by. He put himself through a tough workout in the apartment building's gym, hoping to burn off tension. That helped, but left him restless. A long shower cleared his mind, but the mess of feelings meant he didn't even try to jack off.

Bart picked a dark blue button-down that brought out his eyes, his best jeans, and a favorite pair of cowboy boots. A glance in the mirror assured him that his hair was combed, and dark stubble accentuated his cheekbones.

He drove to the restaurant—a local Italian place that rated well for date night—feeling jittery like he'd downed too many energy drinks. His stomach was so knotted he didn't know if he could eat.

Will he? Won't he?

Bart checked in at the podium ten minutes early. Jon hadn't arrived yet. Bart had made a reservation days before, and the hostess showed him to a table in a quiet corner, perfect for a romantic evening. He ordered a soda and looked at the menu, trying not to fidget or look at his watch too often.

Seven o'clock came—and went. Bart checked his phone in case Jon had texted him about running late, but there were no messages.

By seven-fifteen, Bart felt like he had a lump of lead in his belly. *He's not coming.*

At seven-twenty, Bart left a ten on the table to cover his drink and a generous tip, then walked out, trying not to imagine everyone was watching, knowing he'd been stood up.

Anger felt better than disappointment over the obvious rejection, so he pushed down the hurt and let himself shout and swear on the whole drive back to his apartment, banging on the steering wheel for emphasis.

When the rage passed, what remained felt hollow and empty. *He's gone. It's over. I'm never going to know whether he played me for a fool. Whether he really cared.*

I hope he covers his tracks so well I can't find him. I don't want to see him locked away.

I'll just have to root out what I felt for him and start over. I'll be back in Nashville soon. It'll be like none of this ever happened.

Deep in his heart, Bart knew it wasn't ever that simple.

Three hours later, Bart's phone rang. He didn't recognize the number.

"Bart." The voice on the other end sounded wrecked, but Bart still recognized it.

"Jon. Or I guess I should say 'Ricky Jon.'" He couldn't keep the ice from his tone.

Silence. "When did you find out?"

"Yesterday."

"I'm sorry that I ghosted on you for dinner."

"That why you called?"

"I'm dying."

Wait, what? "Why should I believe you? I'm not one of

your marks. I won't fall for a stupid sob story." *And yet I have fallen so hard, felt so much. This has to be a trick.*

"Believe me or don't—I'll be just as dead. Look at the bright side. You won't have to arrest me."

Ice slithered down Bart's back. "How long have you known about me?" Betrayal felt like a knife in his guts.

"*After* we were together that last time. I swear I didn't know before then."

Part of Bart wanted to lash out, and the rest wanted to nurse a broken heart. *He's manipulating me, playing on my sympathy, tugging at my heartstrings. This is how he makes his getaway.* He didn't, couldn't believe that the man he'd started to fall for was really dying.

"Someone shoot you making your getaway?" Bart knew he was being cruel, but it hurt too much to be kind.

"Cursed. Not that you'll believe me; doesn't change the truth. You saw the media about Osterman? DEA got their own file, and so did a reporter." Jon—Ricky Jon—stopped for a rasping breath. "He was my last one. I was done." He gave a humorless chuckle. "And it turns out, I really am done. Didn't know he had a witch. Got me good. Death spell—can't be fixed."

Bart froze. As a witch himself, he knew dark magic was real. He'd seen people die like that, a slow, painful, inexorable end. Suddenly he wasn't so sure that Jon was playing him.

"Where are you? I might be able to help."

"Don't want to spend my last days in jail. I just couldn't disappear without telling you that I liked you a lot."

I did more than "like" you, Bart thought, holding back the words behind gritted teeth.

"Jon—"

"Don't hate me. I never meant you harm."

"Just wait—"

"Goodbye, Bart." The call ended.

Bart tried to call back, but it wouldn't connect, and there was no voicemail.

Bart paced and ran both hands through his hair. A message told him that the DEA had called to let TBSI know about the detailed information they'd received from an anonymous tipster checked out on every level.

Bart hadn't yet gotten Boward's full buy-in on his *Takes a Thief* proposal. If the deal didn't happen and Bart brought him in, Jon would see prison time even with the best plea agreement.

Except it didn't sound like Jon would live long enough to get booked.

Bart didn't doubt that Jon's call had come from a burner phone, probably already in the trash.

Jon had covered his tracks perfectly, and Bart had the inkling that self-protection included charms and minor magic to throw psychics and other witches off his trail, too little too late for the spell that was killing him.

Jon didn't know about Bart's magic unless the psychic abilities Bart suspected were real.

If I can get to him in time, maybe I can reverse the spell or heal him. He had tried and failed to save Shawn, but Shawn's injuries weren't supernatural. This might go differently.

He can't have gone too far. But how do I find him?

Mick's words came back to him, something Bart had thought was a joke. "He always wanted to run off to join the circus."

Bart sat at his computer. An email popped up from Boward, letting him know that barring the discovery of more serious crimes, they had approval on the deal to offer clemency in exchange for working with the TBSI.

He pushed his tangled feelings out of his mind and focused on a new task, searching on fairs, carnivals, and circuses in a hundred-mile radius of Memphis.

The list was longer than he expected, perhaps because it seemed to be peak season for outdoor events. Bart remembered going to the state fair with friends in college. He had good memories of the rides and food and enjoyed the festive vibe. The whole county fair thing felt slyly rebellious because his pretentious parents would never have understood going somewhere that gave out awards for livestock.

Bart wondered if Mick had taken his siblings to the circus. The outing wouldn't have occurred to the Carmodys. *Maybe his family went before everything fell apart.*

He wanted to be angry at Jon, and here he was feeling sympathetic again. He plodded on, going through the list.

If Jon was feeling the effects of the curse, then he probably hadn't gone farther than a few hours' drive. It took a little over eight hours to go from one side of Tennessee to the other, depending on traffic and road conditions. Bart had a hunch Jon would stick to the more rural areas. Memphis was near the borders with Arkansas and Mississippi, but again his gut feeling told him that Jon would choose to stay in his home state to die.

I can't let him die. No matter what happens between us, he deserves better.

Bart's online searches gave him a quick education in traveling amusement companies, which he would have found fascinating if the need to find Jon wasn't so dire.

He learned that fairs tended to be locally run, although they often brought in vendors and attractions from elsewhere, while circuses were traveling troupes that moved as a unit from place to place, with more emphasis on performances and trained animals and few if any rides. Carnivals were more loosely defined but seemed to Bart to encompass a fair-like event that could either be a traveling company or an annual event.

He's going to pick a traveling troupe. It's too risky for him to stay put, even if he's in danger.

As Bart delved into the lore, the history and culture of circus folks captivated him. The combination of found family, a tendency to attract workers who defied social conventions, and a protective attitude toward performers who might not fit in elsewhere gave him an inkling of why young RJ might have seen the circus as an escape and why Jon would return there.

"Hell, the old-timers even had their own language," he muttered.

Armed with more knowledge, he went back over his list. He eliminated the state or county-run fairs as too stationary. That still left at least ten traveling companies, including Renaissance Festivals.

How do I go looking for someone when I don't have a photo or a real name?

Bart figured that Jon wouldn't use his legal name and might have an entirely different alias. "Jon" was a pretty common name, and Bart couldn't imagine trying to parse through employment records based on that alone.

He resisted involving a sketch artist because he didn't want to set the authorities on Jon before he'd had a chance to find him and perhaps work things out. Then he remembered something Patrick had told him about, a computer program that could make a realistic sketch based in user prompts.

Bart had no talent for drawing beyond stick figures, so he figured it was his best shot since Jon had an uncanny ability to avoid cameras.

He signed up on his personal email for a trial account and downloaded the program. For the next two hours he worked through the instructions and watched as the software refined the descriptors he added, moving from a generic sketch of a man to one which increasingly resembled the man Bart had taken to bed with him.

"There you are," he murmured when the most recent iteration was as good as if Jon had sat for the drawing. "Where have you run off to?"

He printed out a couple of copies of the sketch and dismissed the program, making sure to delete his work. Jon had gone to great lengths to remain anonymous. No matter how this worked out, Bart didn't want to be the one to ruin that for him.

"Time to play hide and seek."

CHAPTER EIGHT

RJ

Four days earlier

*R*J woke, disoriented, and it took a moment to remember why he felt...wrong.

Cursed. Dying.

Thoughts from the prior day drifted back to his consciousness. Passing along the evidence about Osterman to the DEA, OSHA, and the reporter. Hoping that he and Bart might be able to make a go of things now that his quest was at an end. Realizing that Bart was the agent hunting him. The witch's curse. Deciding to seek refuge once again with the circus.

I've got to get out of here.

RJ didn't know much about curses except what he had seen on television, but he figured that he would grow progressively sicker until the end. That meant he didn't have time to go to Key West, let alone the Caribbean or the Maldives. But one destination stuck in his mind.

I need to get to the Carnival of Mysteries. I don't know if they can cure me, but if I'm lucky, they'll take me in. I'll have family for a brief while.

He showered and dressed, packed the rest of his belongings, and left the room key on the table with a note that he was leaving despite being paid through the end of the week. RJ slung his duffel bag into his car and hoped that the carnival hadn't pulled up stakes before he could get there.

It was possible that the traveling company was just a bunch of Goths with a roadshow. But RJ trusted his gut, and it told him that the carnival was the real deal.

He hadn't had another vision, but the last one still echoed in his mind. *Me, dying. Was that part of the curse, or do I get even less time than the fortnight? If someone shoots me, is it Bart? I hope not, for both our sakes. He might do his duty, but I want to think that he felt enough for me that it would bother him. Or maybe I just imagined that he fell for me, at least a little bit.*

The directions led him away from Memphis, beyond the suburbs, to an area that had more open space but was still close enough to attract city visitors. He parked in the lot and looked up at the large banner overhead.

"Welcome Mortals to the Carnival of Mysteries. Expect the Unexpected."

RJ walked toward the carnival grounds. A large archway with a sign that read "Welcome Travelers" marked the way. Red lettering on a black background gave a suitably creepy vibe. A ticket booth just past the archway blocked the path from the lot. Beyond that, RJ could see circus tents, midway booths, and all the trappings of a good-sized faire.

Deep inside, a voice in his mind said, *home.*

RJ hesitated, reaching out with his psychic abilities to see if he could pick up anything supernatural. He wasn't quite sure exactly *what* kind of energy he sensed, but what lay ahead definitely felt paranormal. Oddly, that confirmation made him feel safer.

No fence surrounded the grounds, but as RJ stepped through the archway he felt a frisson of *something* that made him wonder if the carnival somehow chose who could enter.

He didn't expect to find anyone in the booth at this time of day since the carnival opened later, but to his surprise, a man stepped out to greet him. He was about RJ's height with olive skin, dark hair, and black eyes. His clothing reminded RJ of Renaissance Faire garb with a lace-up white shirt, black vest, breeches, and boots.

"Welcome to the Carnival of Mysteries," the stranger said in a soothing, mellifluous voice. "What do you seek?"

RJ squared his shoulders and mustered his nerve. "I'd like a job. I grew up working fairs and circuses. I've got experience with a lot of positions. I'm a good roustabout."

The man met his eyes, and RJ wasn't sure he could pull his gaze away. He seemed to see all the way down to RJ's bones, making him feel exposed, secrets stripped bare.

"There is a place for you here." The man's language seemed a little stiff, or maybe it was an accent RJ couldn't place, as if the stranger wasn't exactly from this place and time.

Well, he's certainly not a vampire since we're standing out in the sun. So I'll take my chances.

"Where do I need to go to interview?" RJ licked his lips nervously. He didn't sense danger or malice from the man, but he knew on instinct that there was something *other* about him.

"No need. I am the owner of the carnival. Permit me to introduce myself. I am Errante Ame."

The formality of his words made RJ half expect the introduction to be accompanied by the sweep and billow of a cape like in Dracula movies.

Not a vampire. But he's something that isn't entirely human—I'd bet money on that.

"Pleased to meet you, Mr. Ame." RJ had kept to himself for so long his manners were rusty. He didn't want to screw this up. "I'm Jon Miller."

Ame regarded him with eyes that seemed to change color. "You've been many people, but that will do. You will be safe here, but it is not your final destination."

RJ wasn't quite sure what to make of that and suspected the man had magic, or perhaps some telepathy. He didn't care as long as he could stay. "Thank you, sir. I'll do a good job. Where should I go, and what would you like me to do?"

"Seek the small purple tent at the end of the midway. Madame Persephone will be waiting for you. You can be of help to her, and she may be of great assistance to you," Ame said.

On one hand, his words were fairly general. But to RJ, they seemed to hold a second meaning, as if Ame somehow knew his truth and his danger.

"I'll go right away, sir. Thank you."

After a few steps, he looked over his shoulder, but Ame was gone. *He must have stepped back into the booth because people don't just disappear. That would be crazy, right?*

Colorful tents and booths lined both sides of a single avenue. Signs, some hand painted and others in neon, advertised performances in each differently-hued tent—acrobats, strong man, trained dog, magician, clowns, juggler, and more. Food counter signs offered turkey legs, corn on the cob, kebabs, and pizza, while artisan booths sold jewelry, incense, candles, and souvenirs. A few booths with games of chance invited passersby to try their luck.

RJ looked around, assessing. Some of the tents looked new. Others were faded and in older styles, making him think of the photos he had seen of the Ringling and Barnum shows of long ago.

Although the carnival had only one long midway, it stretched farther than RJ expected. He spotted a magnificent carousel that took his breath away. Two stories tall and decorated in neon, its animals were carved and painted with such skill that they looked real. Fantastic beasts like dragons and unicorns pranced beside lithe tigers, broad-shouldered lions, and massive warhorses.

In the center of the merry-go-round, RJ glimpsed the steel pipes of a real calliope. Close to one side was a post with brass rings for intrepid riders to pluck from a peg as they passed, something RJ had read about but never actually seen. The ride wasn't running right now, but RJ fancied he could hear the faint strains of the organ playing the "Darktown Strutters Ball," a classic he'd heard with nearly every troupe he had been with.

Across from the carousel, brightly painted swings hung by chains from a central post. As he stared at them, he could have sworn that the designs slowly changed, and he thought he spotted protective sigils worked in among the swirls and flowers.

He walked on, passing more shops that looked interesting, food vendors with additional tempting treats, and a variety of game stands. A funhouse sat across from a tower with a large wooden slide. Farther down the midway he spotted a haunted house attraction that looked so real it made him shiver.

How do they move some of these? They look so...permanent.

I don't think this is an ordinary carnival. Maybe they have a real witch who can cure me.

One booth, marked "Peter Parson's Plentiful Potions," caught RJ's eyes. *Do they work? Could he have something that might help?*

Ame had directed him to Madame Persephone, and from the name, he suspected she was a fortune teller. His first inclination had been to expect a mere performance, but from what he had seen, and the odd feeling that permeated the carnival, he now wondered if she could be a genuine seer. *After all, I played that role in a couple of circuses, and I've got actual abilities.*

Her purple tent sat a bit back from the concourse, perhaps a nod to privacy for those who sought her counsel. RJ paused before entering. The energy his psychic gift picked up felt stronger here, like he had put his toes in the edge of a swift river of power. The magic didn't frighten him; instead, he picked up on a sense of understanding and inquisitiveness.

So far, the Carnival of Mysteries had been less spooky than its poster suggested. From the bright colors to the mix of attractions, RJ felt like he was *home* for the first time since he had left his last troupe.

RJ drew in a deep breath, pulled himself up to his full height, and entered the tent. It took a moment to adjust to the dim light. Swaths of gauzy fabric festooned the tent walls in colors that seemed to slowly shift. The table held a crystal ball and tarot cards atop a silk cloth whose rich colors reminded RJ of saris. He felt certain that runes and sigils had been blind-stitched into the fabric. To the right, a mirror reflected rows of flickering candles grouped on an inlaid credenza like a shrine along with crystals and an old drop spindle.

"I've been expecting you."

The voice startled RJ. A woman emerged from the shadows. She wore colorful flowing robes that fit with the mystical opulence of the tent. Rings glittered on her fingers —silver, onyx, garnet, opal—all valued for protection and enhancing magic. The tent smelled of vervain, mint, and rosemary, more protective plants.

Madame Persephone spoke softly, but RJ sensed the strength beneath. Her features gave no clue to her age, she might have been forty or four hundred.

"How were you expecting me? I just got here."

An enigmatic smile played across her face. "Errante told me, of course. You are where you need to be."

Either these folks were truly supernatural, or they were very good at their con. Having been around carnival folks for more than half of his life, RJ was rapidly becoming convinced that he had entered a place where the normal rules did not apply.

"Come, dear. Sit down. Would you like your fortune told?"

RJ felt frozen in place. "I know my fortune. I'm cursed and dying. Can you change my fate?"

Madame Persephone beckoned, and he joined her at the table. She looked him over closely and then took his hand. RJ wondered if he imagined that a jolt like static electric sparked between them at her touch.

"Gonna read my lifeline? Because I'm guessing it's a lot shorter these days." RJ couldn't help the gallows humor, a way he had always coped under stress.

"So much fear," she murmured, closing her eyes, and RJ wondered if she was downloading his memories or reading his mind. Such thoughts no longer seemed preposterous. "You have endured great loss. Still, you have the heart of a warrior and strive for justice. Someone with strong feelings is looking for you."

Bart. To arrest me.

"The stain of dark magic grips you. If it is not lifted, you will die."

Hearing her validate what he knew shook RJ. *I guess part*

of me was hoping she'd take a look and decide that the witch thing was all in my head. Apparently not.

"Can you break the curse?" He almost didn't recognize his own hushed voice.

Madame Persephone shook her head. "No. I'm sorry. It is not in my power to do so. I can slow its progress in hopes of finding a cure elsewhere. Peter, at the stall nearby, may have a potion that will ease your discomfort—for a while. But I cannot remove the curse itself."

"Can anyone? Is there a way to undo it?" *I don't want to die.*

"This type of dark magic can only be removed by the witch who cast the spell—or in some cases by their death," she told him.

RJ slumped, discouraged. "I don't know how to make him take away the curse. I can't fight him."

She gave him an appraising look. "You have abilities."

"Minor psychic ones. Strong intuition, sometimes I sense things when I touch someone. Good enough for me to tell fortunes at one of the circuses where I worked, but not what I need to do battle with a wicked witch."

He couldn't read her expression. "Small magics still hold power and should not be dismissed. Those who trust in great powers forget this at their peril."

RJ tried to contain his frustration and disappointment. "I'm sorry to have wasted your time." He moved to stand, but a thin-boned hand gripped his arm with deceptive strength.

"Look deeper. I see nothing gone to waste," she corrected, fire glinting in her eyes.

"I still need a job. Mr. Ame sent me here. Please, I don't have anywhere else to go."

She regarded him for a moment in silence and then nodded. "You can help by selling the crystals and charms to my customers after I do their reading. That would be a great assistance. I can set up a space for you on the other side of the curtain. As for the rest, if Errante hired you, then there is a bunk for you, and the food here is good and plentiful."

"Thank you." RJ knew he might not live long enough to prove his worth, but at least he wouldn't die in his car by the side of the road.

"Go to the costumer's shop," Madame Persephone told him. "Tell her that you've just joined us. She'll have clothing for you. You'll want to look the part by the time we open."

"Don't I need to go to the office and fill out forms to get my bunk and a badge?"

She laughed. "No, dear. The carnival knows."

RJ guessed that he should feel creeped out by the carnival's strange workings, but having grown up with circus folks, the unusual felt more normal to him than what he encountered around outsiders.

He left Madame's tent and realized she hadn't told him where to find the costumer. RJ thought about going back to ask, but then he saw the potioner's tent, and figured he could ask both his questions at once.

"Madame Persephone thought you might be able to help me," RJ said when the man inside looked up. Peter had straw-blond hair that stuck out around his head like a scarecrow. That suited his thin build, all arms and legs, with a long neck, a pointy nose, and a prominent Adam's apple.

The inside of the tent seemed larger than RJ would have guessed from the midway. Sunlight shining through the emerald-colored canvas bathed the interior in light the color of new grass.

Wooden shelves held stoppered glass bottles of all shapes and sizes, filled with a rainbow of liquids. Some were clear, others cloudy, while still more seemed to have sparkles of light floating in them, and a few glowed from within. The air smelled of ambergris and anise, with a hint of something medicinal around the edges.

A narrow wooden table sat in front of the back wall of shelves. On it was a large mortar and pestle that looked like they were made of solid obsidian. RJ thought he saw runes and sigils etched into some of the bottles, and a few had a prominent death's head symbol painted on them in red.

"Oh, you're the new guy with the curse," Peter said, like that was nothing special.

"How—?"

"I've been around for a while." Peter shrugged. "If you're here long enough, you pick things up." He gave RJ an assessing but not unfriendly once-over. "Although I don't think you'll be here long enough for that."

RJ felt a surge of panic. *Does he mean I'm going to die that quickly? Or that I'll move on when they've done for me what they can.*

Peter seemed to realize what he said, or maybe he really could read RJ's mind. "Oh, don't take that wrong. I just figured you weren't planning to become a regular."

"About the curse," RJ blurted. "Madame can't lift it, but she said you might have a potion that would slow it down. I don't know how the curse is supposed to kill me, but if it's going to be painful, I'd appreciate anything that makes that better too, please."

Peter bustled around the tent as if RJ wasn't there. He stared at the shelves, lips pursed as he thought, running a finger through the air like he was tracing the bottles without touching anything. He plucked one bottle from its place, studied it, put it back, then grabbed another and set it on the table. He moved with the fine-boned twitchiness of a wren, completely in his own world as he chose multiple bottles, a few tins and selected items that looked like dried flower pods from an antique wooden bin.

"I can't cure you. But I can give you something to help you function until…well, until you can't anymore."

Peter added the dry ingredients one by one to the mortar, including a dash of something that sent up sparks. He muttered a few words that RJ couldn't catch, adding a green liquid that reminded RJ of pond scum.

The potion master carefully poured the mixture into what looked like an empty soda bottle. "How long is the curse active?"

RJ sighed. "The witch said I'd be dead in a fortnight."

Peter nodded. "Well, on the bright side you don't have to worry about getting addicted to this. Take an ounce every night before bedtime. It will help you sleep, ease pain, and should suppress bad dreams."

"Does it block visions?"

Peter frowned. "I can't promise that. Sorry."

RJ pulled out his wallet. "What do I owe you?"

Peter smiled. "Nothing. You can be my runner when you're not helping Madame. I'm the local pharmacy around here for the regulars. Uncommon folks have unusual needs," he added, dropping his voice.

"Thank you." RJ accepted the bottle with both hands as if it were a magical relic.

"Oh, and don't forget this." Peter handed him a plastic dosing cup like sometimes came with cough syrup. "Don't take too much at once, or you might not wake up."

RJ hesitated. "Ever?"

Peter shook his head. "You'd wake up eventually. But it might be later than you'd want. Best not to find out."

RJ asked for directions to the costumer and put the potion in his pocket. He found his way down the long avenue, noticing stalls he didn't remember seeing as he walked in. He spotted a sign above a tent the color of hot chocolate and pulled back the flap.

"Hello?"

"Oh, hello. You must be the new person." A large woman

in full skirts and a corset that accentuated her bosom came out from behind a rack of clothing. She ducked back and emerged carrying a hanger with a cream-colored poet's shirt, knee breeches, high brown lace-up boots and a gold brocade vest.

"These should fit you, and they'll go with that lovely red hair." She ran her fingers through the hair on the back of his head in a motherly way. "Bring out your eyes too."

RJ didn't even bother asking how she knew his measurements. *Maybe they're all telepaths. Or just magic.*

"Thank you. It's lovely."

She beamed. "Such a sweet boy. Sorry you won't be with us long."

RJ wondered if there was a sign floating over his head that said "doomed" that everyone else could see. *If so, it won't be a problem long enough to worry about.*

"Can you please direct me to the bunkhouse? I'd like to get changed and put my things away."

She sent him back down the avenue to an area behind Madame's tent that was clearly the "village" for performers, out of the public eye. Several long white bunkhouse trailers sat in rows.

RJ stopped a man who looked like a fellow roustabout. "Hi. I'm new here. How do I find my bunk?"

The guy looked bemused. "It's the one with your name on it."

RJ blinked. "But I just got here."

"Look for your tag. It'll be there. That's how things work around here," the fellow said. "Welcome to the carnival." He walked off, leaving RJ feeling like he had tumbled into an alternate dimension.

In the years RJ had traveled with fairs, circuses, and carnivals, he had endured all kinds of accommodations. He had frozen and sweltered in tents, squeezed himself into crowded, repurposed RVs, slept in hammocks, and traveled with one memorable group in a caravan of brightly painted retro circus wagons and VW buses.

He looked at the gleaming trailers, impressed that they were so well maintained without dings or damage. Each trailer had a bathroom with two shower stalls and two toilet stalls. Across the way, he saw a big cement block building that looked like a community bathroom and shower facility, part of the park hosting the carnival. Firepits dotted the area between the bunkhouse trailers. A large trailer looked like an overgrown food truck with a chimney and a walk-up window shaded by a big sun tarp. Nearby another big tent with plastic-windowed walls sheltered rows of folding tables and chairs.

RJ ambled down the rows of trailers, and sure enough, his name was on a paper placard slid into a small frame beside a unit. Nothing about the tag looked recent or rushed, matching all the rest although RJ had only been at the carnival for less than an hour.

He tried the knob, and it turned, so he pulled it open. Inside was a clean, fresh, single room with a twin bed, television, small fridge, air conditioner, and storage area. His key lay on a shelf with the TV remote.

This was the nicest place he'd ever stayed. RJ fought back tears.

At least I'm going out in style and not in a fleabag motel. Maybe they'll pour one out for me when they find my body.

He tried on the garb, and it fit perfectly. He was no longer surprised, and he wondered what other marvels the carnival held in store. RJ tucked his belongings under the bed and took the key, then locked up and headed back toward Madame's.

"Better grab lunch before things get busy." The same man he had asked for directions crossed his path once more. "Go to the mess tent. The food's free—and good. All you can eat. It's part of your pay. Take advantage," he added with a wink.

Whatever the curse was doing to kill him, RJ figured he wouldn't help it do its job by starving himself. He stood in line behind a group of people dressed in acrobat's unitards. They bore a family resemblance, and he figured they were the aerialists. A big man with bulging muscles stood behind them, and then a man with a dog at his side. The dog looked preternaturally intelligent.

RJ couldn't see the menu, so he watched what others walked away with on their plates, impressed by the variety. When he reached the front of the line, a stout lady greeted him. Her dark hair formed a widow's peak where it had been pulled back in a bun beneath netting.

"What's your pleasure?" she rasped.

RJ still didn't see a sign, so he blurted, "Cheeseburger with fries, please, and a Coke."

"Here you go." She handed him a tray with his order, and he thanked her. It didn't occur to him until he was seated at one of the picnic tables that the burger was made just the way he liked it with his favorite toppings, which he hadn't specified.

"It's as good as it looks." The same roustabout slid into the seat across from him with a couple of slices of pizza. "Everything here tastes great."

"Thanks for all your help." RJ tried not to let on that the man's repeated appearance made him feel a little spooked. "It's my first day, and I'm still finding my way around."

The other man laughed. "Oh, we know. That's why Errante asked my brothers and me to keep an eye out and lend a hand."

"Brothers?"

"Identical triplets. I'm Bob, and you've met my brothers

Bill and Biff. It weirds people out when they see us together, but it helps a lot with our magic show."

"I've never heard of identical triplets," RJ confessed, feeling better.

"This is the Carnival of Mysteries," Bob said. "Anything's possible."

RJ bit into his burger and realized that it wasn't just good; it was the best he'd ever eaten. "If all the food is like this, I can imagine it's a great recruitment incentive."

Bob shook his head. "The carnival doesn't recruit. The people who need to be here find us. Works better that way."

RJ asked the question that had been on his mind since he met Ame at the ticket booth. "Is it magic? All of this? It has to be, right?"

Bob grinned, flashing perfect white teeth. "Damned if I know. But it's the best troupe we've ever traveled with."

Bob finished his food and excused himself, reminding RJ to just ask him or his brothers if he needed anything. RJ ate the last of his burger and swallowed down the Coke before cleaning up his trash. He looked around, seeing many of the performers whose signs he had spotted on the midway. The rest, he assumed, were riggers, drivers, game runners, and the many others needed to keep a traveling show on the road.

Madame hadn't given him a time to return, but he didn't want to be late on his first day, so he walked back toward her tent. This time, he paid more attention to the shops, attractions, and food booths that filled the midway.

He could feel the rising energy as if the carnival was coming alive for the day. RJ had always loved that feeling, a heady mix of excitement and anticipation that remained as real to him as a carnie as it did when he had been a boy on a secret visit with his big brother.

I wish Bart could see this. The thought appeared unbidden, and his good mood ebbed. *Except that would be a bad thing, because he'd be here to arrest me.*

It doesn't change how I feel about him. And it's not like I've got time to get over him.

He wondered if Bart had dug deeper than the last agent to at least understand the reason for his crimes. Whetherby had been easy to mislead because all RJ had to do was plant false clues that reinforced the old man's assumptions. Although he didn't know how Bart could possibly trace him to his last motel room, RJ had left a few random printouts about businesses that had nothing to do with his quest to throw anyone looking for him off the trail.

We're supposed to have dinner in a couple of days. Has he figured me out yet? Would he have arrested me before or after our date? And what's wrong with me that even knowing who he is, I'm sad about not showing up?

Then again, maybe being in love isn't the worst way to feel at the end. Even if nothing can come of it. Even if maybe he didn't feel the same way. Better to have loved and lost and all that.

Perhaps tonight, if he wasn't completely exhausted, he'd jerk off to thoughts of how that date might have ended, tangled in bed together, riding each other until they were a hot, sweaty, sticky mess. *I can dream.*

"Glad you're back," Madame greeted him when he entered the tent. "Did you find your way?"

RJ resisted his first thought, which took a much deeper meaning than locating the places he had needed. "Yes, thank you. I think I'm all settled in."

She gave a curt nod. "Good. Let me show you the checkout area. I can help more clients if you run the register. Have you ever done this before?"

RJ had handled the till at all sorts of games and rides over the years. "Yes, Madame."

"Good." She directed him to an ornate bronze old-fashioned register with mechanical keys and a lever to record the sale. The decorative scrollwork in the engraved plating seemed to flow from one pattern to another. RJ blinked his eyes, and they stopped moving.

"I will select the crystals for the clients and wrap them in tissue. It's very important not to touch the gems because they will be attuned to the buyer's energy," she told him. "Ask them whether they want to use cash or credit, then ring up the amount. If they're paying cash, the drawer will open. If it's credit, the register will automatically put it on their card."

"How—?"

She smiled. "It's just the way things work here." Madame gave him a look that seemed to see down to his bones. "There's a stool behind the register so you can rest if you need to. I'll have Peter bring you a drink that will be better than coffee," she promised. "And if you feel one of your visions coming on, just go in the back for a bit to lie down."

I never mentioned getting visions.

"Okay. Thanks." Normally, feeling so *known* would have raised RJ's hackles. But he felt oddly safe at the carnival, and Madame's energy soothed his jagged nerves.

Once the event opened to the public, people trickled down the midway, browsing and buying, or ducking into the tents to watch the performers. Since Madame's tent was at the end, it took a while for the guests to get that far. Some immediately turned around and began to make their way up the other side of the avenue, but others paused and then came inside.

RJ watched from his stool behind the antique register in a little alcove. When Madame told someone's fortune, the colors in the gauzy swags seemed to swirl, and he couldn't hear what was said, even though she and her customer were only a few feet away.

After each reading, Madame selected a crystal and held it

up, presumably explaining its purpose to the customer before she wrapped it and pressed the gem into their palm.

"She's wonderful," the first customer gushed as she stepped up to the register while a new client took her place at the table. "Definitely the real deal. You've got a great boss."

RJ smiled and nodded, ringing up the purchase and marveling at how the register worked since he had checked and couldn't find any wires or ports. Something told him that witchy Wi-Fi was involved.

Peter showed up with a cup of hot tea. "Drink this. I should have thought to give it to you before. It will mask the worst of your condition until it's time to take the other potion. I'll bring you one each day." Peter's not-so-subtle head-to-toe glance suggested a silent diagnosis.

"If you take a turn for the worst, Madame will fetch me. Stop by early tomorrow and I'll have things for you to deliver to the bunkhouse," Peter told him, and RJ thanked him.

When Madame sent RJ to get dinner, he stepped out into the lights and sound of the carnival in its gaudy glory. The rides were running, and music from the carousel's calliope competed with the laughter of children. He caught the smell of cotton candy, fresh fries, cinnamon buns, and sweet sausage grilled with onions and peppers, all the scents he remembered from his circus days.

The food enticed him, but RJ knew he had a free dinner waiting. He hurried to the mess hall, hoping that they had spaghetti. When he stepped up to the counter, the same lady passed him a plate heaped with pasta, marinara sauce, large meatballs, and garlic bread along with a drink.

It didn't surprise him when one of the triplets showed up after he took a seat.

"I'm Bill. Bob asked me to check on you. Everything going okay?"

"Still finding my way around, but I like it here," RJ replied.

"I hear you. It's a special place. I'll be sad when our time is up," Bill said.

"You're leaving?"

"Eventually. Maybe in a year or so. The main acts like Madame are permanent, and some of the roadies. The rest of us stay for a while and then move on, like you will."

Bill spoke like he knew about RJ's situation, but RJ couldn't imagine how that would be. Errante didn't look the type to divulge confidences. *Do other people claim sanctuary here? Are the temporary people all running from something—or someone?*

"Can I ask you a question?"

Bill nodded. "Happy to answer, if I know."

"There's no fence, but I thought I felt…something…when I entered. Does that keep bad people out?"

"The short answer—we are *protected* here. I don't know the 'how' and 'why,' so I can't give you the long answer, but if something's chasing you, it can't harm you here. And if Mr. Ame let you in, then you have the carnival's protection."

RJ noted that Bill said "something" not "someone." He wondered if the spell or magic that protected them separated the witchcraft from the witch. *It's not going to be a long-term problem.*

Bill took his leave, and RJ finished quickly to get back to Madame, who acknowledged him with a nod and waved him over to his seat by the register.

By the time the carnival closed at ten, RJ felt the fatigue of the day more than usual, something he chalked up to the curse.

"Go see Peter at eight tomorrow," Madame told him. "Make sure you have a good breakfast first. He'll have potions for you to take to members of the crew and cast, and they'll want them before they start their set-up or practice.

When you're done, come here, and you can help me go through a new shipment of crystals."

RJ thanked her and promised to follow the instructions. He walked toward the bunkhouse trailers, thinking that without the bright lights and neon of the festival, it seemed even darker. A few security lights lit the midway and the cast area, enough to see his way. Even so, the gloom made RJ shiver.

Over the course of the day, his psychic sense had attuned to the energy around him, whether what powered the carnival was magic or something *other*. During the day, that gave an ambiance of fun, giddy excitement, curiosity, and wonder. Now it felt darker—not sinister, but more somber and nuanced, reminding RJ that even good things often had a shadow side.

I have a safe place to sleep and a full belly. It's enough.

He unlocked his cabin and flipped on the light. Nothing had changed, and he found himself letting out a breath he hadn't realized he had been holding. *It's not like I was expecting there to be house elves or room pixies, was I?*

RJ got ready for bed, and crawled under the covers, making sure to take his dose of Peter's potion. *The carnival is more than I probably deserve. I had good reason not to drag anyone else into my crazy life. But I liked the idea of having Bart along for the ride after the jobs were done. I wish he were here with me without the complications. I miss him.*

He intended to jack off thinking of his time with Bart but fell asleep remembering the feel of Bart's lips on his and what it was like to lie together making out.

THE NEXT TWO days went smoothly, running errands for Peter in the morning and handling the register for Madame the rest of the day. RJ began to relax, picking up on the carnival's rhythms and even recognizing cast members and crew.

Bill, Bob, or Biff seemed to appear whenever RJ was alone, which cheered him up. He liked the triplets and spent time after closing sitting at the firepits trading stories of the road. One night he showed off his meager juggling ability. Another evening found them holding a knife-throwing contest, surprising everyone when RJ came in third. He appreciated not being left on his own to think too much.

The nightly potion, and the tea Peter brought each morning to Madame's tent, kept RJ functioning, although he felt the curse like a low-grade infection. He slept soundlessly and didn't remember dreaming.

On the fourth day, RJ woke with the strange feeling that he had forgotten something important. As the last traces of sleep and the potion slipped away, he realized that this was the day he and Bart were supposed to have their date. Despite everything, it made him sad knowing that he wouldn't be keeping the appointment.

RJ tried to push away thoughts of how it might have gone, if circumstances worked out differently. How they could have spent time getting to know each other better over good food and wine, and then gone to a motel to become more acquainted in a whole different way.

He had fantasized about fucking Bart and having Bart fuck him. Both options turned him on, having Bart deep in his own channel or sinking his cock into Bart's prime ass. He knew they would have been spectacular together, the best he'd ever had. And he suspected that some of that lay in their connection being more than a one-night stand, deepening with their growing, mutual affection.

I've got nothing to lose by admitting that I fell in love with him.

I've already lost it all. I choose to believe he cared for me too. Far be it from me to deny comfort to a dying man.

RJ tried not to dwell on the dwindling number of days left, but sometimes the feelings of loss and grief snuck up on him, leaving him morose. Madame seemed to notice and found chores for him, or lent him to one of the other vendors who needed a sudden "favor."

He was returning from one of those errands when he passed the haunted house. It looked exceptionally realistic for a carnival attraction, and even though RJ knew that it had to be as easy to break down and transport as the carousel or the swings, he shivered.

Although the rides and games of chance made RJ nostalgic for all the years he had spent with troupes on the road, he hadn't tried any of them here. He noted that the haunted house was a walk-through attraction, unusual these days. Something about the spooky signage pulled him closer.

The haunted house was contained in a large truck trailer with a front that assembled to look like a ramshackle, creepy farmhouse. Ghosts peered from broken windows, eerie faces poked from behind the curtains, and a spooky soundtrack set the mood.

Before he knew it, RJ was all the way up at the entrance. The ride jockey gave him an odd look but didn't send him away.

"What's in there?" RJ felt a prickle on the back of his neck.

"Only what already haunts you," the attendant said, which didn't sound like the usual memorized patter. "Nothing you see can harm you, but you might be shocked, scared, and surprised."

RJ stepped inside, entering a foyer that had white sheets thrown over furniture, a grandfather clock running backward, tattered curtains blowing in a cold breeze, and the distant sounds of spooky organ music. His psychic senses went on alert, telling him that there was more going on than clever special effects.

RJ thought he heard a voice he recognized, one he never expected to hear again. "Mick?" He hurried on, wondering if he might have a chance to finally say goodbye.

He realized that he had entered alone, odd since the carnival had been busy that day, and it wasn't quite closing time. A door slid open, revealing a corridor with flickering orange electric candles, creepy oil paintings hanging askew, and a chill that grew cold enough for RJ to see his breath, suggesting the presence of real spirits.

The corridor became a maze, leading him through rooms in a mansion fallen into disrepair. In the dining room, a rotting wedding cake graced the table amid long-faded banners and decorations suggesting that a tragedy of some sort had ruined the celebration. The kitchen looked like a blood-soaked abattoir with maggots that appeared disturbingly real.

As RJ moved farther inside, moans and whispers carried from beyond. He started to wonder how everything could be completely contained within a truck trailer because the haunted house seemed larger on the inside.

"Mick?" he called but got no answer.

RJ looked over his shoulder, thinking that he had been gone too long and should just retrace his steps, but doors had closed behind him, forcing his path onward.

Wisps of mist slithered by, cold and damp where they touched his skin. The air smelled of wet dirt and lilies. In the parlor, he saw an open casket with a corpse inside, ready for mourners to join in the wake. The dread that pooled like a rock in RJ's belly told him not to examine the coffin too closely.

"Mick?"

RJ picked up his pace, eager to be out of the haunted

house. He sensed a darkness here that he had not felt in the rest of the carnival, which made him wonder once again about the magic and energies underlying everything.

A tub and sink full of blood in the bathroom looked and smelled far too real. Then the corridor led RJ to a bedroom with a large mirror. RJ saw himself reflected, and behind him, Mick.

"Mick!" RJ said, relieved. "I took care of the warehouse owner. I got your vengeance. Only it all went wrong, and so I'll be seeing you soon."

The image in the mirror moved its mouth, but RJ couldn't hear it. "Mick?"

His brother's image flickered and changed, becoming the dirty cop that refused medical assistance to RJ's mother. The ghost raged and ranted in silence, slamming against the other side of the mirror, trying to break through to menace RJ.

The telltale tremble of energy that preceded a vision shivered through RJ. *Not now. Please, not now.*

His sight faded, and vertigo sent RJ to his knees, clutching his head. *The scene changed in his mind's eye, and the vision showed him what he had seen before—himself, bloody and dying, in a place he didn't recognize. Bart stood over him, bathed in a strange green light, face set toward an unseen enemy. The light flared, and Bart knelt beside RJ, gathering him into his arms. RJ couldn't hear what Bart said, but he looked distraught. RJ had so many things he wanted to say, apologies and confessions to make, but his body wouldn't respond, and then everything turned black.*

RJ came to with a start, jarred out of the vision when a hand grabbed his collar and hauled him to his feet. Disoriented, he flailed, unsure whether the new presence was friend or foe—or one of the attraction's ghosts seizing an opportunity.

"Whoa! Slow down, slugger. It's Bob. Lenny at the front

said you'd been in here too long and sent me to find you. Come on. I'm here to get you out."

RJ didn't know whether Bob was real or a very believable apparition, but he had no desire to linger in the haunted house alone. He let Bob take part of his weight, slipping an arm over the man's shoulder and feeling Bob's arm wrap around his waist to support him as Bob half-walked, half-dragged RJ to a side door he hadn't noticed, a "chicken exit" for those too frightened to finish.

Outside, the fresh air warmed RJ, who realized he was shivering with cold and that his hands were icy. "Thank you," he told Bob, grateful enough for the rescue that he refused to be embarrassed by his collapse.

"What were you doing in there?" Bob asked, curious but not condemning.

"I thought I heard my brother calling me. My dead brother."

"Oh. The ghosts like to play tricks. Sorry about that. Are you okay?" Bob looked worried.

RJ winced. "Sort of. Sorry to be a bother. I just had a *moment* in there."

Bob shrugged. "People do. Lenny's used to it. The ghosts are part of the 'charm,' but not everyone thinks so." He pulled a sports drink from his backpack. "Here. Drink this. Have you eaten supper yet? I was heading to the mess tent. We can walk over together."

RJ appreciated the effort Bob made to reach out and thanked him for his help. After being on his own since he left the festival circuit two years ago, it was nice to have a carnie family again, even for a little while.

Mr. Miller, the circus master who had taken RJ in when he fled the Carmodys, was gone now, and he had lost track of the friends he had made through the years when he cut himself off to do his "vengeance tour." That just left Bart, and after the vision RJ felt his absence keenly.

RJ had to force himself to eat, even though his dinner tonight was macaroni and cheese, his favorite. Bob kept up enough conversation for both of them and didn't look like he minded RJ's minimal responses. Afterward, they walked back to Madame's since Bob swore he was going that way anyhow, and RJ liked the company too much to protest.

"You've been circus folk for a long time, haven't you?" Bob said as they walked the midway.

"Most of my life. Why?"

"Just something about you. I knew you were one of us the first time I met you," Bob replied. "My brothers and I grew up under the Big Top too. Mom sewed costumes, and Dad worked rigging. We weren't with this carnival back then."

He named another outfit, one RJ remembered hearing about. "Didn't they have a bad train wreck a while back?"

Bob nodded. "Yeah. Bunch of people were hurt or killed. Mom died. Dad got injured too bad to keep doing the work, so he retired and moved to Gibtown in Florida."

RJ had heard of the place. "Gibtown" was founded as a place for retired circus and carnival performers, somewhere they could maintain a community with people who understood "the life." While RJ had known about the town for years, somehow he never expected to get old enough to go there. *Just another premonition, I guess.*

"Sorry to hear that."

"It was a long time ago. Biff and Bill and I do okay. We've been here for a while, and we'll probably move on in a year or so. You know how it is," Bob said.

Wanderlust was part of the DNA for performers and crews. Some troupes were good, others were bad, but even the best company couldn't always compete with the need to see what might be over the next hill.

Bob stopped at Madame's tent. "You sure you feel okay?"

RJ nodded. "Yeah, the drink and the food helped. Thanks again." It wasn't the whole truth, but nothing was going to ease the curse's toll.

"Have a good evening." Bob left, and RJ ducked into Madame's tent.

"Sorry I was gone so long." He hurried to take his place at the register.

"I sent Bob to look for you. Had a 'feeling' you might need a hand," Madame replied, as if precognition was no big thing.

"I did. Thanks. I shouldn't have gone into the haunted house."

She gave him another one of her X-ray looks, the kind that convinced him that she could see his bones or read his mind. "People who are close to the Veil often get glimpses because the threshold is thin," she said. "More so when there's native ability. Best to stay away from that place."

By the Veil, she means death. I'm vulnerable to the ghosts, because I'm almost one of them.

"You don't have to convince me." He forced a smile. "I learned my lesson."

The rest of the evening passed quickly with a surge of visitors eager to have their fortunes told. Staying busy kept RJ's mind occupied, although he still noticed when he should have gone to meet Bart and regretted not canceling their date instead of standing him up.

I'll call him tonight and apologize. I was trying to protect myself, but it doesn't matter now. And I doubt he could find me here anyhow.

When the carnival closed, and the music ended, RJ walked back to the bunkhouse, more aware than ever of the energies that swirled through the festival grounds in the darkness. *There's real magic here—and real ghosts. Does it all somehow travel with the show? Maybe the ghosts used to work here and never left. The life gets into your blood.*

He settled into his bunk room and reached for his phone. *I need to leave things as right between me and Bart as I can. Maybe he'll remember me well. One less thing on my conscience. It won't do any good, but I can at least let him know how I feel.*

And if it means I get to hear his voice one last time, it'll be worth it.

RJ mustered his courage and dialed Bart's number.

CHAPTER NINE

Bart

The next day

"*H*ave you seen my brother?" Bart handed a copy of the computer sketch to the man at the fairgrounds' ticket booth. "He's not well, and he's gone missing."

Given the outsider bent of the traveling festival community, Bart thought he might do better looking for a missing "family member" than going in as a law enforcement agent. So far no one had run him off with a shotgun, but the sketch didn't spark any recognition.

The bearded and tattooed man at the desk walked the picture around to the handful of people in the back office and then returned, shaking his head.

"Sorry. We get lots of people through here for tickets, but if he applied for a job, someone would have done the paperwork," he handed the art back to Bart. "Hope you find him."

Bart thanked the man and shuffled back to his car, where

he guzzled some of his coffee and checked the festival off his list.

So far this morning, he had found five of the ten events he had marked as strong possibilities for Jon to seek sanctuary. Bart still thought of him as "Jon" even though he knew it wasn't his full, real name. *We can hash that out if I ever see him again. It's the least of our worries.*

He had put Patrick on the trail of Osterman's witch, Shultz, with orders not to approach if found. As it turned out, others in the TBSI had been eying Shultz for a while without any luck getting solid evidence to convict. A killing curse would be sufficient proof of malicious use of magic, and an attack would be all the provocation necessary for Bart to have clearance to kill the witch in self-defense.

We have to find him first.

According to his dossier, Shultz was suspected of several suspicious deaths and accidents related to Osterman's Freight, but evidence and witnesses were scarce. Jon could be the missing piece, enabling the Bureau to get a conviction—assuming Bart and Shultz didn't first end up in a duel arcane to the death.

Bart didn't mind asking for help tracking Shultz so he could focus on finding Jon. If other agents found Shultz, Bart could confront the witch about the curse he had put on Jon. Time was running out, and Bart knew he couldn't hunt both men at the same time.

He feared that too many agents wouldn't see past Jon's recent rap sheet, even though Bart had arranged for a partnership and clemency. He didn't intend to take any chances with a trigger-happy agent who wanted credit for the capture.

Bart looked at the other traveling troupes on the list, which he had arranged in order of distance. A car matching the description of the one RJ drove for his visit to the

Carmodys had been found without its plate down a dirt road in a rural area that wasn't close to anything. The VIN tracked back to a dead man, whose nursing home belatedly confirmed that his car had gone missing. Not surprisingly, the car had been wiped clean of fingerprints and was uncannily devoid of anything that could provide DNA.

Bart turned the A/C full blast on his face to revive his late-morning slump and gulped more of his coffee before selecting yet another traveling attraction, the next closest by distance.

Jon's words played over in his mind, increasing the urgency. *He's dying. Cursed. If I don't find him fast, it'll be over forever. I've got to track him down, break the curse, save him. I'm not willing to let him go.*

His next destination was a small, dingy circus that looked like it had seen better days. It fit easily in the parking lot of a deserted shopping plaza, with one large tent, a dozen games of chance that looked rigged even to Bart's eye, and a couple of ramshackle rides Bart wouldn't have risked a crash dummy to test. He felt relieved when they disavowed any knowledge of Jon's whereabouts.

To his surprise, the Renaissance festival had a professional business office despite its costumed actors with their dubious accents. Their hiring manager quickly scanned the most recent hires in their computerized system, comparing drivers' licenses with Bart's sketch.

"He might be here as a visitor, but he's not a cast member," she told Bart. "We're also very strict about guests staying with any of our on-site folks, so he'd either be registered here or whoever was hiding him would know they'd be fired if we found out."

Bart trudged back to his parking lot. He ate a drive-through burger and soda in the car and drew a line through the festival's name.

Just three more to go, and I'll have to broaden the search radius. I didn't think he'd go more than a hundred miles, but maybe he was scared enough to put more distance between us.

I wish he'd answer his phone and believe me when I tell him I'm not going to arrest him.

Bart pushed down his worry and drove, following the GPS to the next dead end.

Discouraged, Bart weighed his options. *I like the sound of Carnival of Mysteries, although it's probably just a bunch of Goths with Ouija boards. Still, if Jon really did have some psychic ability, he might have thought he would fit in.*

As he drove, Bart practiced what he wanted to say to Jon once he found him.

I'm not going to arrest you. If you'll cooperate, I worked out a deal so you don't go to jail, and we can be partners hunting supernatural criminals.

Let me try to heal you. I'm a witch too. Maybe I can help.

I think I love you. We'll figure it all out together, and nothing else matters.

Bart wasn't sure Jon would believe a speech like that, but it was the best he had. The more time passed, the more anxious he became. Tracking spells didn't work, and Mick's ghost had nothing more to say. The burner phone Jon had called from had been difficult to trace, eventually providing location coordinates that didn't exist. Bart still didn't know how Jon had pulled that stunt off.

He followed the signage for the Carnival of Mysteries, pulled into the lot, and parked. Even from a distance, the cluster of tents and banners made him uneasy. Bart reached out with his magic, scanning for threats. The results were perplexing.

What lay beyond the archway had an energy Bart had never encountered before. Neutral, but strong without a clear source. The power felt ancient and did not spring from the location itself. Strangely, Bart couldn't read any vibes beyond the carnival's archway, as if a barrier kept him from piercing through.

The strange power didn't seem sinister or malicious, but Bart sensed strains of both light and darkness, and something deeply protective. Beyond that, everything was blank.

If Jon believes he was cursed by a witch, maybe he figured someone at a magical carnival could lift the spell. It's what I'd do in his position.

Bart walked toward the entrance arch, registering a prickle of strange power all around him. He felt a ripple of energy when he crossed the carnival's threshold that he knew would have taken immense power and skill.

Bart decided to stick with the "searching for my missing brother" routine since he had definitely gotten the impression that traveling folks didn't trust the authorities. At first he wondered if anyone was in the booth until a striking man in an outdated costume stepped out to greet him and not-so-subtly block his path.

"Greetings, Necromancer. I am Errante Ame. What brings you to my carnival?"

Bart's eyes widened and reflexes kicked into high alert. Few people would easily pick up that Bart was a witch, let alone recognize his necromancy. He eyed Ame, trying to place the energy he felt. *Witch? Immortal creature? His carnival?*

Clearly, his earlier ruse wouldn't work and might alienate the man. Bart had a strong feeling that the stranger could be a powerful ally—or a dangerous enemy.

"I'm looking for my friend. He's sick—cursed—and I want to help him. He might have come here because he was scared." Bart regulated his energy and protective shielding to let the other man read his sincerity.

The dark-eyed stranger gave him a look that seemed to see his soul. "Your lover, not just a friend. Your connection to him is tangled. I do not give sanctuary lightly. If you mean him harm, leave now."

Bart raised his chin. "I don't want to hurt him. I'm breaking a lot of rules to be here. I care about him, and I have a plan to save him. But if he dies, it's all for nothing. Please, if you know where he is, help me."

Few other practitioners gave Bart pause, but whatever Errante was, his magic was resonant with age and power. Bart felt respect—and a sliver of fear.

"He came to us looking for healing and shelter. We can ease his suffering, but we cannot lift the curse," Ame said. "His time is short. We can offer a safe place among friends to spend his final days and a merciful passing. What more can you provide?"

Bart chafed at the delay. He wanted to shoulder past and turn the carnival upside-down looking for Jon, although he knew that would be a massively bad idea. Yet for as much as he balked at explaining himself to this stranger, the man's integrity impressed him, as did Ame's compassion for a man he had only just met.

Then again, it didn't take me long to fall in love with Jon and decide to risk everything to save him.

"You're right about my magic. I'm sure you can sense my energy," Bart replied. "I love him, and I've found a way for him to keep his freedom. I'm willing to confront the witch that cursed him to fight for his soul. If we succeed, he won't die, and he won't be punished for avenging the wrongs done to his family. I want to see if we can be partners. I want to offer him family and safety. It's dangerous and messy. If we fail…" Bart swallowed, "I will ease his passage to beyond."

Bart spoke his truth as openly and honestly as he knew how and felt his words and magic being weighed in the court of the stranger's gaze.

"I believe your intentions are as you say," Ame replied

after a long pause. "You may indeed find a way to save him. If you betray my trust—and his—know that your power will not protect you."

Bart felt the lick and whisper of strange energy around him, a taste of fire and ice. He felt certain that Ame and his carnival were not people he wanted as enemies.

"I understand. Please, let me find him, and if he will go with me, don't try to stop us."

Ame nodded. "I grant you access. It is up to him whether he chooses to leave. If he prefers to stay—even if it means his death—I will respect that, and you will not force him to go."

The carnival master put Bart's deepest fear into words that Jon either wouldn't trust Bart or had already given up and resigned himself to his fate.

"I won't force him, but I hope to convince him." Bart willed the other man to recognize his sincerity. "I want us to have a life together."

Ame stepped back toward the booth. "Go. Heed my warnings. I wish you well."

Bart turned toward the midway and felt certain that if he glanced over his shoulder, Ame would be gone. He thought again about the power he'd felt when he'd entered. *Did Ame do it all by himself, or is there something essentially supernatural about the whole place?*

Under different circumstances, like a date, Bart might have enjoyed taking in the sights and sounds. The brightly colored tents, rides bathed in neon glow, crisscrossed strings of white bulbs along the midway, and the smell of decadent treats would have been appealing if Jon's life didn't hang in the balance.

The afternoon sun hung low, turning the sky indigo. Ahead of Bart, the carnival's lights glowed, and the faint strains of calliope music carried on the air.

Bart read the signs in front of the main act tents, trying to figure out where he would find Jon. It didn't escape him that Ame had permitted him to enter but did not tell him where Jon would be or hint at his location. Clearly, it was entirely up to Bart to find him and convince him—and hopefully, win his trust.

Bart felt tendrils of other magics reach out to sense him, confirming his suspicion that many of the carnival regulars had special abilities. The wisps pulled back, wary, but did not try to help or hinder. To his magic, the entire carnival hummed with energy.

The haunted house attraction made him slow his step as he felt the real ghosts inside. They skittered away from him, retreating into their stage of metal and glass, wary of his magic. He did not sense malice, so he ignored them. Nothing about the carnival he had encountered so far seemed sinister, but he kept his guard up, still cautious.

At the end of the midway, Bart spotted a small purple tent with psychic energy so loud it nearly screamed in his mind. The ability behind that energy was real and powerful. Bart strode toward the tent, and then hesitated outside the flap.

What if Jon sees me and bolts? What if he won't come with me? If he has made up his mind, can I let him die?

Bart took a deep breath and pushed open the tent flap. Inside, layers of casual magics created an atmosphere of wonder, curiosity, and security—good for trusting a stranger with one's most private questions. From the subtly shifting colors of the gauzy swags to the real power of the divination tools on the table—crystal ball, cards, runestones, bones—he knew the owner was a powerful seer.

"You came." Madame Persephone emerged from behind a curtain. "I worried you might be too late."

"What did you foresee? I can sense your magic."

She favored him with a faint smile. "I've never met a necromancer before. He doesn't know, does he?"

Bart shook his head. "I didn't keep it from him on purpose. We didn't have enough time for it to come up."

Her smile turned to a smirk, though her eyes remained friendly. "I'll bet. I sense the connection between you. Solid, although new. Your energies align, which means your souls have a promising fit."

Bart felt her magic's light touch like fingertips gently mapping out his profile. Taking the measure of his energy, reading his aura, deciding whether he could be trusted.

"I have an idea of where the witch who cursed Jon is," Bart told her. "I'm willing to fight the witch to save Jon, and once the curse is lifted, I think my magic can cure him. If your gift can provide any insight or confirmation about the witch, I'd be grateful."

She nodded with a thoughtful look in her eyes. "I have been scanning for that energy signature since he arrived. I may be able to help." Madame's gaze raked him from head to toe. "Do you love him? Because he is in love with you."

Bart's heart soared before crashing once more back to reality. "Yes. I fell for him against my better judgment, against my will almost. I wasn't looking for 'complications.' I'd had my heart broken when my fiancé was killed, and I didn't think I'd risk that again. Jon made me feel once more. I'm putting my job and my career on the line to save him. And if we face off against the witch, I'll risk my life too."

"He's at the bunk trailer. Under the name Jon Miller," Madame told him. "It has to be his choice to go with you, but if that's his decision, I'll help you however I'm able."

"Have you seen his future?" Bart found himself holding his breath.

"Only glimpses, things that may be or might not, moments out of context. That tells me that it is still fluid— but your time is running out."

Madame gave Bart directions, and he headed into the

backstage area, quickly spotting the rows of large, white bunkhouse trailers. Since the carnival was in full swing with plenty of attendees, the area was deserted. Bart wondered why Jon was in his bunk during the event, fearing he was feeling the effects of the curse.

He found the door for Jon Miller and paused. *Is that a new alias or one he's used before? No wonder we couldn't pick up anything on his real name.*

Bart stood outside, working up the nerve to knock. If he were here to make a bust, he'd have already gone charging in. But he wasn't here as Bart Gibson, TBSI Agent. He'd come to find the man he had fallen in love with, the one for whom he was risking everything, hoping to convince Jon to come with him and live.

Trying to save Jon's life could get them both killed. But losing Jon without doing everything in his power to see where their story together could go was something Bart couldn't live with.

He knocked and realized he was holding his breath.

The door opened, and Jon stood, backlit in the opening.

Just in the five days that had passed, Jon looked haggard. He had dark circles beneath his eyes, and his light complexion looked sickly pale.

"Jon," Bart breathed.

Jon greeted him with a pained smile. "Hello, Bart. Actually, I prefer RJ." He sighed, and his shoulders slumped. "Can I grab my stuff before you cuff me?"

Bart's eyes widened. "I didn't come to arrest you J—RJ. I've got a plan to save you—and maybe us. Will you hear me out?"

Bart had never needed tact and diplomacy more than right now, something he had often been accused of being short on when he was focused on a job. Now he feared RJ might be too skittish to believe or too hopeless to seize the possibility.

RJ stood back, letting Bart enter, and closed the door. The bunk room was a tight fit for two large men. Bart wedged himself into a corner while RJ sat on the bed.

"Why did you look for me? I'm a dead man walking. Nine days left," RJ told him in a matter-of-fact tone that made Bart grind his teeth. "They said they'd give me a good end here. I'm no danger anymore. Please, just let me go in peace."

"Do you *want* to die?" Bart tamped down his fear and frustration. "If there was a way to break the curse, is that still your choice?"

RJ's expression and posture told Bart the other man was tired, maybe in pain from the dark magic. "Of course not. I wanted to run off to Key West or the Maldives. And before it all went sour, I had this crazy dream of taking you with me." His sad smile broke Bart's heart.

"That part's not so crazy." Bart gentled his tone, wishing he could hold RJ in his arms for this conversation. "What's probably nuts is that I started falling in love with you from the beginning. That's real. I've worked out a way for you to cancel any criminal charges by being my partner at the Bureau. They approved it—you'd be off the hook, and we'd be together. But you need to stay alive."

RJ barked a bleak laugh. "Yeah, that's the hard part. Got any ideas?"

"I'm a necromancer," Bart blurted. "Errante at the gate knew right away, so did Madame Persephone."

"Can you heal me?" Hope sparked in RJ's eyes.

"I can't break the curse, but afterward I can sustain you while you heal," Bart told him. "We're closing in on the witch. Madame said she'd help. I'll fight him to the death to save you. Just please, RJ, don't give up on getting better. On living. On us."

Bart knew he wasn't great at putting his feelings into words, but this was his best shot, being as open and honest as he could muster. He could have used his magic to nudge RJ toward a decision. *Hell, I could tamper with his soul. But I won't. This has to be his choice.*

"What if it doesn't work?" RJ looked up at him expectantly and licked his lips nervously. "If it goes wrong will you bring me back here for the end and stay with me? They've been good to me. At least I'd be among friends."

Bart's heart was in his throat. "I will do everything in my power to keep us from getting to that point." His voice broke, but he didn't care what it revealed. "But yes, if it comes to that, I will."

"How did you find me?" Curiosity shone in RJ's eyes.

"Mick told me you liked circuses," Bart replied as if conversing with a ghost was commonplace. Sensing that RJ wasn't going to try to run, he slid down to sit on the floor with his knees bent in front of him.

"Mick? My brother?"

Bart nodded. "Necromancer, remember?" He told RJ how he had pieced the clues together, finding the real names in the foster care record and following the trail to understand the tragedy that ripped the Tucker family apart.

"Did you find my sister, Kit?"

Bart hated to disappoint him. "No. I tried, but no one answered. She might still be alive—or she's somehow unable to hear or answer me."

"I want to believe she's out there and okay, even though I know that's probably not true," RJ replied with a sad smile.

Bart glanced around the bunk room. "This is a nice place. I never knew what went on behind the scenes with these shows."

RJ's expression softened. "Mick took me to the circus a couple of times when he could scrape the money together. I loved it. When I ran away, I found a troupe that would take me in. They gave me a new name, taught me all kinds of things, paid me fair. I worked with one traveling group or another until about two years ago when I left to work my plan."

"You mean, get payback for what the people did to your family?"

RJ nodded. "Circus is found family, at least the best ones are. So when everything went wrong on that last job with the curse...I came to the place I knew would take me in."

"I'm sorry I didn't know about the curse right away, that I wasn't there to protect you," Bart said. "But I'm here now. And I won't leave unless you send me away."

RJ swallowed hard and looked away. "I missed you. But I was afraid when I found out you took over for Whetherby, and I didn't want you to be ashamed of me. I couldn't have stood seeing the disappointment in your eyes—or hate."

It took all of Bart's control not to move closer to RJ and touch him. "I was angry and hurt at first because I thought maybe you'd played me."

"No. I swear—"

"I know that now," Bart hurried to put in. "But that's where my head was when you called. I had just figured everything out about why 'Ghost Boy' picked his targets and put in my proposal to work out a deal to drop the charges when I realized you were behind it all. It took a little getting used to."

"Ghost Boy?" RJ smirked.

"Shut up," Bart said without heat. "That was Whetherby's name because he couldn't find any clues to figure out who you were. Great job on that, by the way. That's half of how I got the brass to see your value as my partner."

"Oh yeah? What was the other half? My incredible blowjob skills?"

Bart felt his stomach unclench. If RJ was talking to him, joking about sex, maybe they had a chance.

"Definitely not. Those are 'need to know' only," Bart teased back. "You documented your evidence better than half the agents in the Bureau. Accurate, readable, thorough. Good writing skills may have saved your ass."

"Nice to know." RJ's smile faded. "Can you forgive me? I never really lied...I just didn't tell the whole truth." He suddenly looked scared and much younger.

"I didn't exactly run my plan to rescue you through channels," Bart admitted. "I got the okay on the partner deal. But I'm off the grid right now. Rogue. If we succeed in taking Shultz out and saving you, we're heroes.

"If not, I'm out of a job, my career's in the crapper, and without you...I'll have lost it all." He met and held RJ's gaze to get across just how much of a commitment he had made. "There's nothing for me to forgive. Can you trust me?"

RJ held out his hand. "Until my dying day," he said as Bart took hold.

"Not funny," Bart warned.

"Gallows humor." RJ pulled him close for a kiss, with Bart on his knees between RJ's legs. Bart slipped his arms around RJ's waist and RJ cupped the back of Bart's head with one hand, stroking his hair with the other.

The kiss started slow and gentle, and it felt to Bart like they were saying with their hands and lips everything they hadn't been able to put into words. He drank in the scent and heat of being wrapped up in RJ, greedy for more but knowing that they had to take it slow.

"I know it's crazy, but I think I love you," RJ confessed, separating just enough to speak, leaving their foreheads touching.

"Funny thing—I think I love you too," Bart replied in a

husky rasp. He reprimanded his cock for wanting to move things along.

They kissed a while longer, letting their hands and mouths relearn the map of each other's bodies before RJ leaned back.

"What's next?" He let his fingers tangle in Bart's hair and slid off the bed. Bart turned so that RJ sat between his legs with his back to Bart's chest and their arms wrapped together.

"Patrick, my research assistant, has been adding files to an online folder, everything he's finding about Shultz and where we might locate him. I dug up plenty of information about curse breaking before I came looking for you. I have some ideas, but I'm hoping Madame can add to them," Bart told him.

He hesitated, fearing the answer to the next question. "How do you feel?"

RJ paused. "At first, it was like when you know you're getting sick, but you aren't yet. I could tell something wasn't right. Mr. Ame, the carnival owner, knew right away when he saw me. So did Madame and Peter—the potions guy."

"Potions?"

"Yeah, just like in the movies, except he's the real deal. Oh, I guess I should tell you I've got some psychic abilities. I can't read your mind, but I'm really good at picking up on unspoken clues from people, guessing their next move, and I can sense energy."

"I figured you had some sort of talent," Bart replied. "It probably helped us 'click' so well."

"Anyhow—potions. Peter mixed up a tea and an evening drink for me that he says slows the curse, but it won't hold it off forever. One perks me up to keep going through the day, and the other helps me sleep deeply and not dream," RJ filled him in. "I think they help. So if we leave here, I want to ask for some to take with me."

"Absolutely. We need to get Madame's help before we do anything," Bart agreed. "What else do you feel from the curse?"

"Each day, it's a little more. I can tell that I'm running a low fever. I've got a headache that never goes away, I tire easily, and my joints ache when they shouldn't. Like the flu coming on, but not exactly," RJ said. "Sometimes it hurts to breathe. Food doesn't taste good. There's always something new like it's all adding up until the end."

Bart squeezed him tight. "We're not going to get to that point," he murmured close to RJ's ear.

RJ squeezed him back. "I'm expecting that as the days go by, it'll become more painful. It seems like that sort of curse. From what I learned about the warehouse, everyone was afraid of Shultz and what he could do."

"That would fit," Bart agreed, although he hated the thought. "Apparently the Bureau's had him in their sights for a while, but this is the first time we've had witnesses—and ghosts—who can testify. With the warehouse shut down and Osterman in custody, Shultz will run. I've got some ideas where he might go."

Bart rested his cheek against RJ's ginger hair, taking in his scent. He loved the way it felt to hold RJ close and stroke his hands and forearms. RJ leaned back against him, and Bart sensed relief, surrender, and acceptance.

"Madame sent me back to 'rest,'" RJ mused. "I bet she knew you were coming."

"She and Errante Ame both said they expected me," Bart replied. "They also made it clear there would be hell to pay if I let you down. Which I have no intention of doing. I'm in this all the way."

They sat together for a while longer, and Bart took in the

rhythm of RJ's heartbeat, the cadence of his breathing, the smell of his shampoo. Yet beneath all that, he could pick up a sour note of sickness in his sweat, and Bart's magic tingled a warning about the touch of dark power.

"Madame will expect me back," RJ finally said, stretching. He gently broke Bart's hold but pressed a kiss to his knuckles in apology as he freed himself. "If she's not ready to talk to us, maybe you can wander around and take in the sights. It's not like any other circus."

"I'm sure you pick up on more than most people since you're psychic," Bart said as they got to their feet. "With my magic, it's pretty trippy. I can see where the energy overlays what's real and makes it *more*. I'm surprised I've never heard of this carnival before."

"I think they manage to stay low-key. Or maybe the people who find it are the people who need it."

The small room didn't leave much space to move around. Bart opened his arms, and RJ walked into his embrace, settling his hands on Bart's hips. Bart wrapped his arms around the shorter man's shoulders. RJ rested his head on Bart's chest, and Bart held him close. It was apology and forgiveness, reassurance given and taken, acceptance and belonging. When they finally separated, Bart felt a flash of loss.

"The Bureau doesn't know you're here?" RJ asked as they walked back to Madame's tent. They matched strides effortlessly, bumping shoulders occasionally.

"No. I turned off GPS on my phone and in the car. I checked for a tracker on the Vette—there isn't one," Bart replied. "There's no manhunt for you. You aren't Public Enemy Number One. Boward's trusting me with loose reins."

"Good. Because I don't think a bust would go over well here," RJ replied with a hint of mischief in his eyes.

"Yeah, I can't see that happening. And if Shultz is looking

for you, he's not going to get past the wardings. I'm pretty sure Ame made an exception for me," Bart said.

The midway still bustled with attendees who crowded into the shows, waited in line for the rides, and dug into the food trucks' treats. For just a moment, Bart could imagine being at a fair like this on a normal date, kissing on the Ferris wheel, winning a prize for his boyfriend, sharing a funnel cake.

Someday, when this is all over.

They stopped outside of Madame's tent. The a-frame sign read, "Closed for a private reading."

"Let me check," RJ said. "I know she told me to come back this evening."

"Maybe we *are* the 'private reading,'" Bart said.

RJ poked his head into the tent, then gestured for Bart to join him. "You were right," he said as they entered.

Madame beckoned them to her table. "Good. You found each other. That's the first step." She gave them an approving once-over. "Now, we must find the witch who did this."

"Do you have a lead?" Bart was afraid to get his hopes up. Before stopping at the carnival he had checked the shared folder that Patrick had been adding to all day, glancing at the contents long enough to see plenty of background on Shultz but precious little information about where he might be right now or how to stop him.

"Magic leaves traces," Madame replied. "This witch has some power, but he sounds sloppy, likely overconfident. That works in our favor." She had moved her crystal ball and Tarot deck to one side. In their place lay a map of the state and a crystal pendulum hanging from a clear glass base like a planchette.

"Give me your hand." Madame traced a shape with one finger on RJ's palm and then took it between her own. "I'm going to try to follow the thread of his magic to the source."

She fixed Bart with a look. "Your job is to watch the pendulum and notice where it moves."

Madame closed her eyes and hummed quietly. RJ looked to Bart, who gave him a nod of reassurance. Bart had seen locator magic before, and while he didn't know anything about Madame's training or path in the Craft, he knew good spell work could get results.

For several minutes, both Madame and RJ sat quietly, eyes closed. Bart chafed at the delay, impatient for results. His eyes grew wide when he saw the crystal pendulum tremble. The movement grew more pronounced, and the carved stone started to swing—slight movement at first, then more pronounced, unmistakable motion.

Bart knew that none of them were causing the motion directly. He kept careful watch on the map as the pendulum moved back and forth as if searching for something. It stilled, hanging at an unnatural angle from its support, and the sharp end of the crystal pointed directly at the little town of Quito.

Abruptly, the pendulum fell back to neutral as Madame and RJ opened their eyes, and she broke the connection by letting go of his hand.

"Well?" She looked at Bart.

"It pointed to Quito. That's a very small town, but we can hardly go yelling for him in the street."

Madame gave him a dour look. "Of course not. You want to lay the trap for him to come to you. You enter his space, and he will know it. He'll wonder why the person he cursed has followed him and fear retribution. He'll sense your necromancy and worry. His kind is too vain to run away. And when he comes to strike, you strike first."

Bart's first impression of Madame Persephone had been of a plump, comforting auntie. But as she laid out a battle plan, he saw shrewd intelligence in her eyes, a firm set to her mouth, and a crafty expression that suggested that she—like the carnival—was much more than she appeared.

"We don't know anything about Shultz's training or his type of magic," Bart said. "I wish we had more information."

Madame huffed. "Can you sense the curse? What does it tell you?"

Bart had avoided probing too deeply since his reunion with RJ was so new. Now, with a nod of permission from RJ, he stretched out his magic without touching, letting the flat of his palm hover above RJ's forearm. He closed his eyes and focused his attention inward.

"I can sense the darkness and the...poison...for lack of a better word." Bart parsed through the sensations. "It's potent, but it feels messy. Like hitting someone with a sledge-hammer instead of running them through with the point of a sword."

"Yes," Madame agreed. "We can work with that. Sloppy spells have weaknesses. Elegant spells can be watertight. What else?"

"He's not a necromancer. A necromancer has a direct connection to death. Their spell would be like an assassin's strike. From the 'shape' of the spell, it feels cobbled together, made up of bits and pieces. It makes me wonder if he's self-taught or picked things up from various teachers without real training. That makes it more difficult to unravel because it's like a ball of tangled barbed wire."

Madame nodded. "The only sure way to end the spell is to force the witch who cast it to remove it. Some spells and curses break with the death of the caster, but some don't—which is an insurance policy for the witch." She glanced at RJ. "He will need to be present. You want the power of the curse to snap back to the caster when the spell is lifted, removing it from the target. Too many things can go wrong if there's distance between them."

"I'll be fighting a witch to the death," Bart protested. "How can I keep RJ from being in the line of fire?"

"You will have to be careful. Any spell or relic I might give you to repel magic is likely to interfere with the breaking of the curse," Madame warned. "But I do have some pieces that might help."

Madame removed a few objects from beneath the table. "Errante left a few things for you." The first was a velvet pouch. "This contains wing bones of a Caladrius to speed healing once the curse is lifted."

Next she held out a silver dagger to RJ. "You know how to use a knife?"

He nodded.

"This blade will attune to your abilities. When you throw it, focus with your gift as well as your eyes, and it will fly true."

The final item was a piece of parchment covered with fine script and symbols in flowing brushwork. She tucked it back into its envelope. "This is an illusion script. Speak a word of power to activate, and the spell will make it difficult for your opponent to fix your position in his mind. It doesn't last long," she warned, "but it might be enough to give you first advantage."

Madame went on without a pause. "Peter sent enough of the potion and tea to take care of you for a while. He wishes you luck."

"The carnival doesn't involve itself directly in disputes, and we cannot allow anything to draw danger to our people or our guests," she told them. "And yet, Errante feels strongly that justice be done. So you go with our blessing. And if for some reason your fight goes badly, come back and we will care for you."

"Thank you." RJ looked desperate and grateful. Bart echoed his gratitude.

When they left the tent, the carnival had closed for the night, and the rides were dark. Without the lights and music, the shuttered attractions and closed tents loomed ominously in the twilight.

"Guess we should get my things." RJ looked pensive. The midway was deserted enough that Bart chanced a quick squeeze to RJ's hand.

"What's wrong?"

"I know I can't hide here when there's a chance to be healed. I want to be with you. But for the few days I've been here, I felt safe," RJ admitted.

"You found sanctuary," Bart said. "That's rare and precious. But it's not meant to be home."

It didn't take much to gather RJ's few things from his bunk room. To his surprise, Biff was standing outside.

"We'll keep your name on the room until everything's settled," he said. "In case you need to return. Mr. Ame will know. Good luck."

They didn't encounter anyone else as they walked through the empty midway. Bart didn't sense danger, but he felt *observed*. They didn't belong to the carnival, and while it had provided shelter, Bart strongly doubted they would ever return.

They threw RJ's things into the trunk when they reached the Stingray, the only car remaining in the empty lot.

"Where to?" RJ asked.

Bart reached over and took his hand as he steered out of the lot and back to the road. "Tonight, we'll get a place to sleep. Tomorrow, I'll see what Patrick sent me and check whether a few other sources delivered what I asked for. We'll make plans. And then we go hunting for that damned witch."

CHAPTER TEN

RJ

*B*art found a mid-price chain motel not far from the carnival that offered clean rooms and a big enough parking lot that the Vette didn't stand out.

"Is this a date?" RJ teased in the elevator. "The motel is way nicer than what I usually picked."

"It's absolutely a date because I'm not using my expense account," Bart joked back.

The cookie-cutter room had a king bed, television, desk, armchair, and a bathroom with a shower large enough for two big men.

"It's late. Why don't you get cleaned up for bed—*sleeping*," he added with a pointed look. "I'll ward the room."

As RJ collected what he needed, Bart put down salt lines at the doors, windows, and vents, and then traced invisible symbols on the walls to hide their magic and keep them free from prying eyes.

RJ flashed a grateful smile and disappeared behind the door. He heard Bart moving around in the next room while he ran a hot shower and slipped under the water, wishing he could wash away the worry and the curse.

Bart came for me—to help, not to arrest me. I was afraid to hope. No matter what happens, we'll be together.

It didn't take him long to finish his simple routine and take his nightly dose of potion. When he emerged, the room was darkened except for a lamp on the right side of the bed where Bart sat against the headboard with his laptop propped up with pillows.

"I don't need the light on, but I figured you'd rather not fall over anything." Bart had pulled aside the covers on the other side of the bed and patted the spot next to him. "Come to bed."

RJ wore a T-shirt and briefs. He crawled in beside Bart and pulled the sheet over him. Bart turned out the light so that only the dim glow of the computer screen remained.

"I'm having a hard time believing this is real, that you're here with me, and we're back together," RJ admitted in the dark.

"It is, I am, and we are." Bart reached out to pat RJ on the shoulder, proving that he was not a figment of his imagination. "I'm going through everything Patrick sent me so we can get a jump on this tomorrow." He shifted a few inches closer and ran his fingers through RJ's hair.

"Shultz probably isn't expecting you to come after him, and he has no reason to expect us to team up. We're the bait for the trap, but we don't want to spring it until we have everything in place," Bart went on. RJ resisted the urge to throw his arm over Bart's lap and press his face against his boyfriend's hip.

"Got a place in mind?" RJ realized he sounded as groggy as he felt. "Because having a witch war here at the motel seems like a bad idea."

"Agreed. I've located a couple of spots that might work,

but I was hoping I'd get a clue from the stuff Patrick uploaded to explain why Shultz would fall back here. From what I can tell, he was raised in this general area, so when he's not hiring himself out to someone, this may be his home base."

"If the locals know he's a witch, they might be too afraid to cross him. He's probably banking on that," RJ murmured.

"You're probably right. I'm not expecting any local help. But I am looking for a nice, abandoned barn somewhere on the edge of town where we can stage a throw down," Bart said as he scrolled through options.

RJ found that he couldn't keep his eyes open. "G'night." He snuggled against Bart as his eyes dropped closed.

"See you in the morning," Bart said softly.

RJ roused once in the middle of the night to find Bart still intent on his screen. When he woke again in the morning, he smelled coffee and saw that the computer had been moved to the table.

"Did you sleep?" RJ frowned.

Bart brought him a cup and gave him a once-over that felt more clinical than sexy. "I slept enough. I've also got a spot picked out for our showdown. I'm glad I had everything we'll need in my bag—there's nowhere close that has these kind of supplies.

"I picked up breakfast pastries for us. Once you're dressed, I want to scout the barn I found before Shultz realizes we're here. I've got a couple of charms that should hide our magic long enough for that. After the barn is set up, we come back and flaunt ourselves without the charms, hoping that Shultz picks up on it and wants to know what the hell you're doing here and who the witch is that's trespassing in his territory."

Bart took a bite of his croissant and followed it with a few gulps of coffee.

When they headed out, they left the "Do Not Disturb" sign on the door, and Bart added a touch of magic to make the housekeepers ignore the room.

They were quiet on the way to the barn. RJ tried to sort through his tangled feelings. Happiness, relief, and surprise that Bart had found him and still cared about him. Worry over the confrontation with Shultz, fear that the curse might not be lifted, and dread that Bart might get hurt or killed defending him.

"Stop thinking so loud," Bart joked. "We'll be okay."

"It's just…a lot," RJ confessed. "Have you fought another witch before?"

Bart hesitated a fraction longer than RJ liked. "A few. Witch fights are like bar brawls. Each one is different. There are things I can do as a necromancer that regular witches can't—I'm hoping that gives us an advantage."

The old tobacco barn stood in an overgrown field of weeds and wildflowers a few miles north of town. By the look of the barn's bowed roof and faded paint, no one had bothered with it for quite a while. Gray weathered boards showed the wear of storms and sun, warped and splintering. The doors gaped open like a dark maw.

Inside, it smelled of mildew and old hay. Bart had brought two high-powered lights to make sure there were no surprises, but gaps in the siding left enough light through to enable their inspection. Nothing remained of the barn's former use besides some rusted implements and a broken-down antique tractor.

Bart stood in the center and turned in a slow circle, taking in the possibilities.

"You really think Shultz will come here?" RJ asked. "Why not ambush us at the motel?"

"He could—but that would be too public. There's a difference between rumors of a local witch and eyewitnesses or video footage. Bible Belt folks are pretty serious about driving out the devil, but at a comfortable distance. It's one thing for Cousin Joan to think she sees the face of Satan in her breakfast toast and another entirely to have two witches dueling with magic on Main Street," he added.

Bart pulled a can of spray paint from his bag, shook it, and strode over to the corner farthest from the doors and well-removed from the rusted equipment. RJ watched as Bart used the paint to draw a circle about eight feet across and then added symbols RJ didn't recognize.

"As soon as Shultz gets here, you jump into the circle and stay there." Bart's tone didn't allow for argument. "Make sure you don't smudge the lines, and stay away from the edges. You need to remain completely inside the marks—that includes arms and legs. He can't use magic on you when you're in the warded area."

"I feel like a damsel in distress," RJ said, bothered about being the fought-over prize.

Bart moved next to him and raised a hand to gently touch his cheek. "More like the unarmed civilian caught between two mercenaries. It's not an insult to your manhood, which is very nice." He gave an exaggerated glance to RJ's crotch, lightening the moment.

"I can't use all my concentration in the fight if I'm worried about protecting you," Bart admitted. "I need you here with me to draw Shultz out and break the curse, or I'd have left you safe at the carnival and come after him alone. But he'll try to use you against me as a weakness, and we can't afford that. We don't know what he's capable of."

RJ swallowed his pride and nodded. "I just don't like you taking all the risk."

Bart kissed him and smiled. "Babe, you're the one with the curse. That's enough risk. And just in case, you've got the blade Madame gave you. I hope you don't need it, but keep it handy."

"What does the circle do?"

"It keeps out magic. Shultz can't cast a spell on you or hit you with a fireball. He can't cross the lines once they're activated—but neither can I. It's a witch-proof zone. You should be safe."

"Can't you make other runes to power up or hit him with a sneaky spell, like in the movies?" RJ asked.

Bart shook his head. "Anything that would strike at his magic will null mine as well. I'm afraid we're stuck with an old-fashioned O.K. Corral-style duel with spells instead of six guns."

With the circle marked, they headed back to the car. RJ felt pensive and nervous, uneasy with the barn and the idea of the fight. Moving too quickly made him dizzy and his stomach hurt, all likely effects of the curse. He would have preferred to strike from a distance instead of putting himself and Bart in direct danger.

"Quit brooding," Bart said as they drove back toward town. "No matter how we confront Shultz, it will be dangerous. This way, there are fewer people in the line of fire, no one for him to take hostage to force our hand."

"We just go into town, let ourselves be seen, and then go wait for him in the barn?" The plan felt too simple. He would have preferred more elaborate subterfuge. "You're gambling on him not wanting to blow his cover. What if he doesn't care?"

"Then we've got problems," Bart admitted. "But think about it—if he jumps us in public, not only could it end up being caught on video, but the cops could get trigger-happy. A regular bullet might not kill either of us, but it could tip the odds of who wins the fight, and I don't have a Kevlar vest for you."

"It just seems like a performance more than an ambush."

Bart considered for a moment. "In a way. Magic has its theatrical side, and old customs die hard. But I don't have his phone number to invite him to parlay. He may think we want to bargain. And if we're wrong about his whereabouts, he might not show up at all."

They stopped at a convenience store for snacks, chatting up the cashier about being new in town and looking for things to do. At the gas station, Bart and the guy at the next pump talked sports cars and gushed car details over the Vette. Instead of keeping a low profile at the diner over lunch, they chose a seat at the window, flirted harmlessly with the server, and were visible enough that everyone in the restaurant was aware of their presence.

At each stop, RJ casually mentioned looking for "an old friend" and dropped Shultz's name. Every time, the person clammed up with a frightened expression and suggested that they abandon their efforts to "reconnect."

"I've spent years flying under the radar," RJ griped quietly as they left the diner. "Paying cash. Not calling attention to myself. Hats and sunglasses. Now I feel like I've got a target on my back."

"We do," Bart agreed. "On purpose." He frowned and gave RJ a second glance. "When we went out for dinner before it all blew up, you had cut your hair and shaved your beard. Was that for a job?"

RJ nodded. "Yeah. I went clean-cut and dark-haired for the Carmodys, and blond when I put spy cams in the warehouse."

"A man of a thousand faces," Bart joked as they drove away. "I'm partial to the way you looked that first night in the bar—shaggy red hair and enough beard to give me rug burn in all the right places."

"I will keep that in mind," RJ promised, appreciating Bart's efforts to stop him from worrying.

When they got to the barn, Bart parked to the side in a copse of trees, hiding the car as best he could. RJ saw him frown with concentration and guessed he was using his magic to sweep the area, on alert for Shultz to be lying in wait.

"Stay close," he warned as they got out of the car.

RJ reminded himself to breathe. He tried not to clench his jaw and hoped he didn't lock his knees and make himself faint. Working one of his jobs to con a mark was different from confronting a killer witch.

Last night the curse bothered him more than he had let on to Bart. Even with Peter's potion, the fever and nausea were growing worse. RJ swallowed some ibuprofen when Bart wasn't looking because every joint ached, from his big toe all the way to his neck and shoulders. When he directed his attention inward, RJ sensed a growing number of things that weren't right.

He had a headache that never completely went away. His appetite was gone, and food didn't sit well when he forced himself to eat—something completely out of character. The potions suppressed bad dreams, but vestiges of their horrors lingered when he woke, slipping away like wraiths, leaving him disquieted.

More than once, RJ wondered what madness possessed him to leave the safety of the carnival on what he snidely—and silently—had started thinking of as his "farewell tour." He knew as soon as he saw Bart that he would do whatever he could to be with him for however long it lasted. But even more, he never wanted Shultz to be able to use his curses on anyone else.

One final hurrah.

The barn looked just like it had when they left. Bart

struggled to close the sagging doors then hurried to the painted circle and inspected it carefully, touching up a few spots.

Just as Bart stood from that task, the barn doors slammed open. Shultz stood silhouetted in the entrance.

"Go!" he told RJ, and Bart slapped the paper with the illusion script onto his own shirt. RJ leapt over the painted marks into the safety of the circle.

The script gave Bart first mover advantage, and he sent a blast of power that threw Shultz against the barn wall with enough force to make the wood shudder in protest.

A ball of green fire sizzled as it hurtled toward Bart once the illusion broke. He knocked it away with a twitch of his fingers, and it sputtered into nothing.

Shultz got to his feet. "You shouldn't have come."

"Yeah, well. We're here." Bart raised his right hand, palm out, and an invisible force shoved Shultz back again. "Remove the curse, and I'll let you live."

"You're here on account of that piece of trash?" This time, Shultz sent a blast of flame at Bart like he had aimed a torch. Bart brought his palms together, and the fire went out without setting the barn around them ablaze.

"Lift the curse," Bart commanded.

"No."

This time, Shultz's magic fire burned toward RJ, but when it tried to cross the painted circle, it flared against the invisible barrier and dimmed to embers without causing any harm. RJ took a step back on reflex, holding the silver knife in his clenched fist.

RJ wasn't sure what he had expected of a duel between witches. Movies showed a lot of dramatic backflips, flying and hovering, and fiery swords. Neither Bart nor Shultz ever left the ground. Sometimes RJ couldn't see the actual struggle since it looked like an epic staring contest, although his psychic abilities felt the warring energies.

"We're not the only ones on your tail," Bart told Shultz. "The Bureau knows about you. Osterman will rat you out to get a plea deal. I'll give you a chance to surrender. Other agents won't."

"They can't touch me—and neither can you," Shultz sneered. Twin streaks of fire, one from each hand in opposite directions, pointed at the old wood and piles of debris, igniting it and turning the air hot and acrid. When Bart shifted his attention to put out the flames, Shultz gestured, and the beam overhead broke with a crack like thunder, sending down a hail of wood and shingles.

RJ threw the knife, and it sunk hilt-deep into Shultz's shoulder, breaking his assault on Bart.

At the same time, Bart's magic flung the largest pieces of wood out of the way, tossing them against the far wall.

"Bart!" RJ shouted, unable to see his partner for a few seconds amid the dust. He threw his arms over his head to fend off the falling pieces that rained down on him even within the circle.

Too late, RJ realized that some of the debris had fallen across the painted lines of protection.

RJ heard metal screech and looked up in horror as Shultz's power tossed the old tractor at him as if it were a toy. It skidded across the boards, ripping up the wood as it went, tearing into the painted circle. Before RJ could dodge, a sharp piece of rusted metal sliced into his side. Blood gushed, running through his fingers as he pressed against the wound.

RJ staggered. Shultz laughed.

"No!" Bart roared. He wheeled on Shultz, thrust his hand out, and clenched his fist.

RJ thought Bart lifted Shultz from his feet by his shirt.

But it looked like Bart's hand went *inside* the witch's body. It might have been a trick of the light or RJ's fading senses, but he could have sworn he saw both Shultz and his ghost in Bart's grip.

"Break the curse!" Bart commanded. He twisted his wrist, making the witch and his spirit cry out and writhe in unison. RJ would have been frightened if he weren't half-dead.

"He's bleeding out. Save him, or kill me," Shultz laughed through blood-flecked lips.

Bart shook him, stretching body and soul farther apart. "I can leave you like this until you die. Or I can make it quick. Break the fucking curse!"

Shultz paused but a moment more, and Bart stretched farther. The witch screamed out the words to the counter curse.

RJ felt the effects of the spell vanish immediately as he dropped to his knees, too dizzy and weak stand.

"Go to the abyss," Bart snarled at Shultz. He tore the ghost free from the witch's body and hurled the mangled spirit and Shultz's corpse into a black portal that opened out of nowhere and vanished immediately.

"RJ!" Bart ran, catching him as he fell forward. He rolled RJ onto his back and pressed a hand against the gash to staunch the flow of blood.

"The curse is gone, but it's not going to matter," RJ managed. His heartbeat slowed, breathing took effort, and he felt a growing coldness. The wound in his side didn't hurt so bad anymore, something he knew wasn't a good sign. After everything, he'd come this far just to die.

"Stay with me," Bart commanded, investing his words with magic.

"I'm sorry," RJ murmured, feeling himself slip away. "I love you."

"I won't let you go." Bart laid his hand over RJ's heart. "Do you trust me?"

"Always." RJ struggled to draw a breath, and his heartbeat stuttered.

This is the vision—me, bloody, dying in Bart's arms.

I don't want to go.

RJ felt a strange energy fill him, spreading from where Bart's hand lay on his chest. He sensed Bart's presence in his mind, and it felt like Bart's soul wrapped tightly around his own.

"I've got you," Bart told him, and while his voice was calm and in control, RJ saw fear in his lover's eyes.

"Necromancer, remember?" Bart replied to his unspoken question with a strained smile as his hand shifted and RJ felt the bond between them tighten. "Your body is dying, and I can't heal you fast enough to stop that. So I'm holding onto your soul to keep you from drifting away while I fix what's wrong."

Being not-quite-dead meant RJ could still see what was going on, but his body refused to respond to his control. He remembered all the movies where someone's ghost had stood next to their bedside, looking down at their own corpse, and realized it was an accurate portrayal.

Bart's magic—or maybe his soul—felt like a strong, comforting presence that took away the cold and dulled the pain. RJ couldn't hear actual thoughts, but he felt Bart's emotions washing over him, and wondered if he was lucid enough for Bart to sense his in return.

Love, worry, fear...calm, competence, stress. In this place between life and death where RJ hovered, tethered to Bart's spirit, it was hard to tell their thoughts apart.

Bart murmured an incantation, and RJ sensed something intangible "snap" into place, binding them together. Only then did Bart move the hand splayed on RJ's chest so he could gently pull back the torn cloth of his shirt from where the metal had sliced into him.

"There's no way to get an ambulance here in time," Bart said, and RJ wondered if talking eased Bart's stress or if he knew RJ's spirit might be able to hear him. "Once I've gotten you stabilized, we're going to get you to a doctor and make sure you've had your tetanus shot."

Bart's hand slipped inside his shirt and covered the bloody wound. RJ felt pressure and heat, but he was too weak to cry out at the pain.

"Sorry. No time for niceties. You've lost too much blood already." Bart's tone had shifted from panicked to dispassionate like a doctor. "I'm going to use my magic to get you out of danger."

The hand on RJ's side burned like a branding iron, down through skin and muscle. RJ thought he could almost *feel* the torn tissue and organs knitting back together as magic accelerated the closure far more thoroughly than stitches.

Bart's expression tensed in concentration, color draining from his face as he poured energy into the magic.

Finally, he sat back on his haunches, looking haggard and exhausted. Bart reached a blood-covered hand into a pocket and brought out the velvet pouch Madame had given them, the bones to speed healing.

"I hope there are instructions," Bart joked weakly. He opened the drawstring and found a yellowed parchment. A moment's study led to Bart dumping the Caladrius bones into his palm and then pressing them against the angry red line that remained on RJ's skin as Bart spoke the words of power from the parchment.

Fire blazed through RJ's body, racing down every vein and artery, burning along his nerves. He felt the warmth of new blood replacing what lay puddled beneath him. RJ gasped as his spirit slammed back into his body, no longer an observer but an active participant in the fight for his survival.

"Almost," Bart whispered. "Just a little more."

RJ wanted to tell him it was working, but unconsciousness overtook him, and everything went black.

CHAPTER ELEVEN

Bart

*T*he fight was a clusterfuck right from the start.

Bart knew Shultz was closing in moments before the barn doors slammed open. He shouted a warning to RJ but couldn't watch to make sure he got to safety. The illusion script bought him a single strike before the effect was lost, and he and Shultz faced each other in a fight to the death.

If it hadn't been for the curse, Bart would have struck fast and fatally, ripping Shultz's soul from his body before the lesser witch knew what was going on. But killing Shultz without ending the curse was too risky—and might destroy RJ's only chance of surviving.

So Bart bided his time, trading blows, trying to keep Shultz from immolating them. Shultz had to know he was outgunned magically, so bringing down the roof was his only real option—and it worked.

In the seconds it took Bart to keep from being crushed beneath the roof timbers, Shultz hurled the rusted equipment across the broken warding. Bart saw a sharp edge slice deep into RJ's side, nearly impaling him.

The look of shock on RJ's face and the gush of blood would haunt Bart's dreams forever.

He reacted with fury, unleashing raw necromancy against Shultz, who never stood a chance against Bart's more powerful magic.

He knew that some traditions in the Craft would condemn what he did, ripping the soul from a living person and casting it and the body into the darkness of the Veil. He knew from Shultz's treachery that he couldn't let the witch live. In that moment, Bart didn't care about judgment or consequences.

Break the curse. Save RJ.

He had wrung the counter curse out of Shultz then eliminated the threat, but it cost precious seconds while RJ bled.

He's dying.

Bart's magic knew how much the curse cost RJ, making him acutely aware of the steady drain on his lover's life force.

Now, RJ's slowing heartbeat and labored breathing thundered in Bart's enhanced hearing. He could see the fading glow of RJ's life energy and smelled his blood.

"RJ!" Bart shouted, and RJ looked up at him with an expression of pain and shock before he fell.

The curse was gone, but the fight to save RJ's life had just begun. Bart knew he was fading too fast to call an ambulance or get to a hospital. A glance told him that the damage would require not just magic but necromancy if RJ was going to survive.

RJ confessed his love, a goodbye. Bart refused to stop fighting, but he needed RJ's consent for what came next.

He had heard soul anchoring called a dark art. In the wrong hands, it could be misused. But to Bart it was a tool just like emergency interventions at the hospital. While his magic stopped the flow of blood, Bart used his own life force, coupled with his power, to tether RJ's soul, holding body and spirit together.

He had never worked this type of magic, but Bart refused to let RJ die when he knew his lover wanted to live. He wove the strands tighter to bind them closely enough that if Bart's efforts failed, they would both die.

No one else is dying today.

Knowing that RJ's spirit was probably aware, although his body had shut down, Bart kept up a running commentary, as much for his own sanity as for RJ.

Bart wasn't a trained healer, but since necromancy dealt with the threshold between life and death, he could use those similarities to his advantage. He let his magic sweep through RJ's unconscious form, cataloging the failing systems and the extent of the injuries. Bart wound his power more tightly where RJ's body was giving out, willing the spark to remain.

A healer knew how to relieve pain and studied the most elegant ways to knit torn flesh back together. Bart used the brute force of his magic to repair the damage, fusing flesh and muscle, replacing blood, relieving the strain of shock. Bart added the Caladrius bones once he had stopped the bleeding, letting their power overlay his efforts.

It was the difference between surgery on a battlefield or in a safe suburban hospital, but Bart had run out of options. He did what he could to suppress the pain, but had to focus on saving RJ's life.

When the wound was healed and Bart sensed RJ's blood volume had returned to safer levels, he sat back on his heels. His hands and forearms were soaked red, and between the battle and the healing, Bart felt like he was running on fumes.

RJ was out cold.

"Probably for the best," he muttered. Bart stood, then bent

down and hefted RJ into his arms in a bridal carry as gently as he could manage.

"Need to feed you better. You're getting skinny," Bart added as he made his way to the Vette. Bart didn't doubt that the strain of the curse was responsible and made a silent vow to stock up on groceries to put meat back on RJ's bones.

Bart would report the situation once he figured out where he and RJ stood with Boward and the Bureau, and whether they needed to hide until the situation sorted itself out or if it was safe to come in.

Bart weighed his options before he drove away from the barn. RJ still needed a doctor, but going to an Emergency Room would raise too many questions. For one thing, Bart still wasn't clear on RJ's legal ID and didn't want them to end up arrested. On top of that, he had closed the wound well enough with magic that explaining the injury to a civilian doctor would sound crazy.

Which meant breaking a few more rules.

Bart found the contact in his phone list and waited for a familiar voice to answer.

"Bart? Is that you? How bad is it?" Doctor Hal Horton was part of a vanishing breed—a rural doctor in solo practice. Semi-retired, stubborn as a badger, and well-aware of things that went bump in the night, Horton had patched Bart up more than once under dodgy circumstances when he needed to keep an injury off the books.

"Hi, Hal. This time, it's not me, but...fuck, it's bad." Now that RJ was out of immediate danger, the adrenaline high was fading, and Bart knew just how close he had come to losing him. *Might still if I missed something.*

"Talk to me."

Bart left out the details of the case, explaining that his new "partner" had gotten skewered by a rusty piece of farm equipment and the emergency measures Bart had taken to keep him alive.

"I can see the headline, 'Necromancer Practices Medicine Without a License,'" Hal replied with dark humor.

"RJ probably needs more blood," Bart said. "And a tetanus shot or whatever you do for that sort of thing, plus you need to check to make sure I didn't leave anything still bleeding inside. Oh, and he was cursed so he didn't start out in the best shape."

"You sure do like a challenge, don't you?" Hal said. "Bring him in. How did you fare in all this?"

"Scrapes and splinters from the fight. I'm pretty wrung out from using so much magic."

"Then I have two patients," Hal surmised. "Any other mojo I should know about?"

"I tethered his soul with my life force, so if he dies, I die."

Hal was quiet for a moment. "When you said 'partner'…"

"Yeah. It's new. And complicated." Bart hadn't unwound the lines of power that bound them together, fearing that RJ might yet take a turn for the worse. He felt RJ through their bond, sensing the rise and fall of his chest, the beat of his heart, and the level of his discomfort.

"He's still in pain, and I don't know why," Bart confessed. "This was field surgery, not anything fancy. I'll never be a threat to your job."

"Do you know his blood type?"

Bart wasn't willing to hazard a guess. Magic didn't always line up with modern measurements. "No."

"Okay. I'll get some O negative. I have a neighbor who can come right over to donate. Anything else I should know? Aside from the curse, any allergies? Chronic conditions? Transmissible infections?"

"Nothing that showed up to my magic," Bart replied. "For what it's worth."

"From you, it's worth a lot. I can do some quick tests to be sure once you're here. Is this an official visit, or are you coming in the back door?"

"I honestly don't know," Bart admitted. "We're staying off the grid for now."

"You sure do know how to put your foot in it," Hal said. "Okay. Come in the back way, and I'll keep things off the books. Cash is good—cash and top-shelf whiskey is even better. How far out are you?"

"About forty-five minutes," Bart replied. "I might be able to shave some off that, but it would be a really bad day to get picked up for speeding."

"Just get here in one piece. I'll be waiting."

Bart could sense RJ's vital signs through his magic, but that didn't stop him from checking multiple times. RJ still looked pale, and he groaned and shifted in pain without regaining consciousness.

"Not much longer," Bart said, although he doubted RJ could hear him. "We're almost there. Gonna patch you up— you'll be just fine."

Bart trusted Hal, but that didn't stop him from worrying. He parked at the back of the doctor's house and pulled his gun before he stepped out of the car.

Hal came out on the porch. "It's clear. Get inside."

Bart apologized under his breath as he carried RJ inside, automatically heading for the examining room in a back bedroom set up for situations just like this.

"Put him on the table, and then scrub up," Hal told him. "I'm going to need a nurse."

Hal was gowned, scrubbed, and gloved before Bart got RJ situated, and he hurried to comply.

"Help me get his shirt off him so I can see what's going on." It took both of them to maneuver RJ, but they managed to cut off the ruined T-shirt and flannel. They left his blood-soaked jeans since the wound was above his hip.

Bart stepped back and waited off to the side, trying to stay out of the way while Hal did his assessment.

"I knew this little sonogram unit would come in handy." Hal wheeled the machine over. He switched it on, added some gel over the thin pink scar where the damage had been done, and moved the wand over it slowly, eyes glued to the screen.

"What are you seeing?" Bart asked, unable to remain quiet.

"You did a good job of closing the wound. Since I don't know the antiseptic properties of magic and you didn't have the proper equipment to flush it out, I'm going to put him on intravenous antibiotics and give him a tetanus shot, as well as an anti-toxin," Hal said. "I don't see any internal bleeding, but I'd like to keep him under observation, at least for the night. I'd ask for longer, but I know not to push my luck."

Bart was too worried to retort. "How is he on blood?"

"Down a pint or two, I reckon," Hal replied. I've got a transfusion waiting for him. Since he can't tell us how he feels, and you said he was poorly going into this, I'm going to hook him up to all the monitors I have, just in case."

"I'll sit with him."

Hal cocked an eyebrow. "You're not looking too good yourself right now. Once I get him set up, I'm going to give you a once-over." He held up a hand to forestall Bart's objection. "Nope. You want me to treat him; I treat you too."

"Fine."

It worried Bart to see RJ so still and hooked up to so much equipment. He still hadn't released the anchoring energy that bound them together, taking reassurance in being able to monitor RJ's condition in his own way.

"Now, let me have a look at you." Since RJ was on the only table, Hal had Bart drag a chair under the bright lights.

"Get hit on the head?"

"Not this time."

"Ingest or inhale anything that might be a problem?"

"Dust and smoke."

"Any open wounds?"

"No." Bart tried not to fidget.

"You mentioned splinters. Show me. Those little buggers can turn nasty if they get infected," Hal said.

Small slivers of barn wood fell to the floor as Bart shrugged out of his shirt.

"You weren't kidding. Almost looks like you tangled with a porcupine. Since neither of us has anywhere to go and nothing to do except watch your friend, I'm going to try to pull these out of your tough hide." Hal reached for tweezers and a bottle of rubbing alcohol.

An hour later, Hal declared him splinter-free, having removed a disturbing amount of wood bits from Bart's skin and scalp, including a couple of needle-thin pieces that had lodged ominously close to his right eye. The rubbing alcohol stung like he'd been attacked by bees.

"I'm going to make a shopping list for you, and you're going to get everything on it when you leave here," Hal said as he cleaned up. "That includes an antibacterial body wash for you, antibiotics for him, and a few other necessities. I'll throw in some pain medication, just in case."

"Thank you." Bart knew he sounded ragged. "I didn't know who else to call."

"Nice to know I still earn my keep." Hal chuckled as he stripped off his gloves, dispensed with his gown, and opened a cabinet, withdrawing a bottle of bourbon and two shot glasses.

"Strictly medicinal, of course." He grinned and filled the

glasses, holding one out to Bart. "Down the hatch." Hal knocked his back. Bart did the same a second later.

"I see you haven't slowed down any," Hal observed after he refilled their glasses.

"That might change." When he wasn't worrying about RJ, other thoughts filled his mind, like what getting involved in a long-term serious relationship would mean. Once the new arrangement with RJ was official, at least they would travel together as working partners. That would be a big improvement. "I love the work, but I get tired of living out of a suitcase."

"Might be easier to handle with the both of you in it together."

Bart sipped his drink. "I imagine so. And he's used to moving around. He's done it pretty much his whole life. But it could be nice to have a cabin somewhere for when we're done."

Picking out curtains for a hideaway in the woods was jumping far ahead, but it tapped into thoughts Bart had pushed aside for a long time. *First, let's get RJ to wake up and pull through. Choose curtains later.*

"I'm going to make a sandwich." Hal stood and stretched. "Want one?"

Bart realized he was hungry. "Yeah, thanks. Anything is fine. What about RJ?"

Hal glanced at RJ's still form. "Let's get him 're-sanguinated,' hydrated, and medicated. He'll be okay for now. I don't want to mess with trying to feed him when he's like this."

Bart pulled his chair up next to the table when Hal went out to the kitchen. He took RJ's hand in his. RJ always seemed full of energy with more than a hint of mischief, so seeing him quiet and pale was wrong on many levels.

"The doc's got you all fixed up." Bart hoped his partner could hear him even if he couldn't respond. He reached out with his magic, doing his own assessment, and couldn't decide whether to be content that RJ was much the same or worried that he hadn't already improved.

"I'm right here," Bart continued. "I'll be with you all night. So just get better. We've got a lot of catching up to do."

Bart wolfed down the sandwich when Hal came back. "Sit with him and holler if anything changes. I've got chores to do, but I'll stop back now and again to check on him," the doc said, taking the empty plate with him.

Bart got comfortable in the chair, still holding RJ's hand. Sometimes he talked about movies or shows he'd streamed, anything to fill the silence. When he tired, he read a magazine someone had left nearby and dozed.

At suppertime, Hal returned with a plate of spaghetti for Bart. "Any change?"

"Should there be? He's been…quiet."

Hal checked RJ over. "I gave him a sedative along with the painkiller to help him rest. The human body is capable of amazing things when we don't get in its way. From what you've said about the curse before his injury, he's been under a lot of stress, and that plays fuck-all with a person's immune system. I've taken care of any worry about tetanus, but that doesn't rule out everything."

He took back Bart's empty plate. "If he gets restless, it might mean the pain meds are wearing off. A fever is definitely a sign something's wrong. I want to know about both of those right away. I'll be in shouting distance if you need me."

Bart left just long enough to wash up in the bathroom, wearing the clean T-shirt and sweatpants Hal set out. The pants were too short, but he didn't care. Just washing off the blood, sweat, and dirt made him feel better, although he could still sense the drain on his magic, even after rest and food. It would take several days after a normal expenditure of power to recharge, and the barn fight, saving RJ's life, and maintaining their bond was anything but normal.

He settled into his chair beside RJ, grateful for the blanket Hal left for him. "Sleep tight," he mumbled. "I'll be right here."

The house was dark and quiet when Bart jolted awake with an insistent panic deep in his gut. He reached out for RJ, who murmured feverishly. Bart touched his forehead. *Definitely too warm.*

"Hey doc! We've got a problem!"

Hal hurried in a moment later, bleary-eyed and disheveled, but he snapped to alertness as soon as he eyed the monitors.

"Fuck. If he's running a fever, there's an infection somewhere. I'll switch up the antibiotic, increase hydration, and hope we can knock it out before it gets worse." Hal bustled around the small treatment room, which impressed Bart, given the man's age and the hour of the night.

"I haven't let go of him with my magic," Bart told him. "I'm not a healer. I don't know if my magic can fight his infection."

"You keep him anchored. I'll do the healing. This is exactly why I was worried, what with him being run down before he got hurt." Hal rummaged in a drawer and returned with a syringe of something he added to one of RJ's IVs.

"Go in the bathroom and grab a couple of washcloths," he told Bart. "I'll get some ice packs from the freezer. Start wiping him down with a cold, wet cloth. We'll get ice at his pulse points. That should help until the drugs kick in."

Bart hurried to fetch the cloths and ran them under cold water, wringing out the excess. "Come on, RJ. I already know you're hot stuff—you don't have to prove it like this," he joked, sounding desperate even to his own ears.

He wiped down RJ's face, neck, chest, and arms, and then repeated the effort with newly-cooled cloths. Hal came back with ice packs for the major pulse points where blood flowed close enough to the surface to be cooled. He turned on a fan and adjusted the air conditioning.

"Now, we wait for the meds to work." Hal dragged another chair into the room. A few minutes later, he returned with a pot of tea and two cups. "Damned if I'll get back to sleep tonight. Might as well make the best of it."

Bart dozed, but his dreams were full of recriminations for not finding RJ sooner, not intervening more quickly with the curse. In the hour of the wolf, the self-blame felt real, although it would not hold up to the scrutiny of day.

Hal shook him awake, and Bart was surprised to see it was light outside. "Have a look at your boy. The fever broke. I'm hoping this means we've turned a corner—in the right direction."

Bart stood, taking RJ's hand again and finding him much cooler than before. Even better, some color had returned to RJ's cheeks, and his skin looked less dry.

"You done giving us scares?" Bart carded sweat-damp hair back from RJ's forehead. "Time to wake up soon. We've got places to go and people to see. And doc here wants to go back to hosting those wild parties of his," he added, just to hear an amused harrumph from the older man.

"You're about thirty years too late for that, but thanks for the thought."

Two hours later, RJ stirred. Bart gripped his hand. "Come on. Wake up," Bart urged.

"Bart?" RJ blinked several times and moaned when he tried to shift.

"Take it easy. You're still hooked up to stuff," Bart cautioned. "But you're on the mend."

"Where?"

"Not a hospital. We're safe. I had a friend who could lend a hand."

"Curse?"

"It's gone," Bart assured him. "But you had a run-in with a tractor that laid you up. It's a lot better now."

RJ squeezed Bart's hand. "Thank you."

Bart glanced at the monitors. He had spent enough time in hospitals to have a good idea of how to read them. All the indicators were better than before, and his magical assessment told him that RJ was nearly out of danger.

"You skipped a couple of meals while you were out." Bart tried to keep his tone light despite his worry. "Think you could eat a sandwich or some soup?"

"I'll try."

Bart left him just long enough to call out for Hal. The doctor hurried in, looking more presentable after a shower, shave, and change of clothing.

"Glad you're back with us," Hal told RJ. "You gave us both a scare." Hal checked the monitors, adjusted the IVs, and double-checked RJ's temperature. "Looks good. I think you're out of the woods."

Hal went to get food. RJ waited until the doctor had left the room before he turned his head toward Bart. "Shultz?"

Bart's expression hardened. "Dead. You don't have to worry about him ever again."

RJ managed a wan smile. "Thank you for saving me. You did something with your magic, didn't you?"

Bart shifted in his chair, unsure how RJ would react. "You were dying. For a couple of seconds, you were actually dead. I knew you wanted to live, so I used my necromancy to anchor your soul to mine and keep you alive until we could heal you. Then I used magic to do as much healing as I could and brought you to the doc to take it from there."

"Our souls?"

Bart knew he was giving RJ a lot to digest all at once. "It's not permanent. At least, it doesn't have to be," he fumbled to explain. "Sort of like 'buddy breathing' in scuba diving when someone's oxygen tank runs out. I shared my life force with you until you were out of danger and held onto you with my magic." He didn't mention that he had yet to undo the spell.

"I thought I was imagining that you seemed so close to me," RJ said. Bart helped him sit up to sip water to ease his dry throat. "I could swear I felt what you were feeling."

That level of vulnerability made Bart shift in his chair. "Sorry about that. Didn't mean to overshare. There's no way to connect like that and keep up walls."

RJ twined their fingers together. "I like it. I'll miss you when it's gone."

Bart grinned and leaned forward for a kiss. "I'm not going anywhere. When you're back to normal, if you really want some sort of bond, there are options that aren't quite so invasive. There's plenty of time to talk about that later."

Hal came back with a tray of food. Bart and the doctor helped RJ sit up to eat, and Hal unhooked some of the equipment, making it easier for RJ to move around.

"What about the Bureau?" RJ asked after he finished his food. "Are you in trouble? Are they still after me?"

Bart carried the tray back to the kitchen and came back to sit next to RJ's bed. "I shouldn't be in any real trouble. Boward knows I was going radio silent looking for you, so I didn't disappear—I've just stayed quiet a little longer than he might have expected. Patrick was sending me updates, and while he promised not to volunteer what I was working on, he'd answer if they asked directly. So technically I didn't go rogue. And I can produce the ghosts of people Shultz killed and let them testify, so any questions about that should be covered, assuming anyone would even ask."

"Except for the part about me."

Bart shook his head. "Boward got sign-off on making that deal we discussed, so there's a way to keep you out of jail, bring you into the Bureau officially, and pair us up as partners. The downside is you'll have to fill in the blanks on your background and go through training."

"I know there will be a lot to learn about the Bureau, but I do have an online degree," RJ said. "Took a lot of classes on law and law enforcement to plan out my 'tour.'"

"That'll help. But you'll have to drop the aliases."

"Jon Miller's not my birth name, but it's been my legal name since I was fifteen," RJ replied. He winced. "I used a real birth certificate, but it wasn't mine. I did it at first to stay away from the Carmodys. Later, once I got the idea of getting back at the people who caused all the bad stuff, I figured it would be easier not to be connected to 'RJ Tucker' so I could disappear afterward and go to the islands."

Bart grimaced. "There are definitely a few complications in that story, but nothing WITSEC hasn't done. It's amazing what can be swept under the rug if the brass wants your help bad enough."

"They'll let us stay together, right?" Fear shone in RJ's eyes for a moment.

"I made myself clear on that," Bart told him. "And Boward gave me his word." He cleared his throat. "And I was planning to ask you to move in with me, since my apartment in Nashville is big enough for two."

RJ's bright smile made Bart's heart melt. "Really?"

"I know you're used to moving around all the time, and we'll still have a lot of travel with the job, but that way we have a home base together in between." He wasn't sure how his nomadic boyfriend would take the idea of settling down. *I'll save the cabin in the woods fantasy for later.*

RJ looked happy but teary-eyed. "I haven't had a real home since my folks died. I want to make one with you." He yawned. "If we don't have to worry about being dragged off in a SWAT raid, can I go back to sleep for a while?"

Bart laughed and leaned in to press a kiss to his lips. "Sleep as long as you want. I'm pretty sure Hal would like to have us hang around for another day to keep an eye on you. In the meantime, I'll go earn our keep and lend a hand around the place."

RJ caught his sleeve before he could turn away. "Don't… let go…of me yet. My soul. Hold on a little longer. Please."

"I can't sustain this forever—it was an emergency maneuver—but I can keep the bond for a while, until you're stronger. So go to sleep. I'll be in the other room—and right here," he said, placing his hand on RJ's chest. "Closer than the Holy Ghost."

CHAPTER TWELVE

RJ

Six months later

"*P*ass the sunscreen," RJ set his Mai Tai aside.

Bart snickered. "I've got a better idea. Why don't I do it for you? I promise not to miss *any* spots."

"Mmm…sounds good. Just remember that applying it to some *spots* in public might get us arrested," RJ retorted. "And I don't want to besmirch my newly un-smirched good name."

"I have something else to slick up those spots back in the room." Bart gave RJ a heated look.

RJ lay face down on his lounge chair. The hotel pool glittered just a few feet away, and steel drum music played over the speakers. Attentive servers brought fresh drinks whenever their glasses ran dry.

I actually made it to Key West—and I'm not alone and on the run.

The only way this could be any better is if we found Kit. But I haven't given up hope yet.

Bart sat down beside him and smoothed lotion over his back and shoulders, making sure to get his neck and ears, slipping his fingers under the waistband of his swim trunks.

RJ gave a satisfied groan. "If I'd have known going straight could be like this, I might have avoided a life of crime."

Bart snorted. "There's nothing 'straight' about it." Since RJ could still feel a delicious ache in his ass where Bart's cock had been just that morning, he agreed.

"True. That's my favorite part of celebrating. We should do some more when we get back to the room." RJ gave a contented sigh as Bart added massage strokes to the sun screening.

"I'm 'up' for all the celebrating you want to do, Intelligence Analyst Tucker."

After RJ filled out all the paperwork, finished the background check, and submitted the transcripts for his coursework, he and Bart had been pleased to discover he qualified for an entry-level Intelligence Analyst position. Boward assigned him as Bart's dedicated partner, which freed Patrick for a promotion. Over time RJ had the opportunity to work his way up to Special Agent, like Bart.

Bart and RJ took the week off between RJ's graduation and his upcoming swearing-in ceremony to spend time on the beach, checking off a big item on RJ's bucket list.

"There are so many ways I can think of to celebrate, none of which can be done on a public beach," RJ replied.

"There's plenty of time before dinner. After dinner too. Not to mention, pre-breakfast," Bart said. "I've got lots of ideas."

Bart's fond tone and his lingering touch made his feelings clear, as did the trace of magic that still bound their souls together. It was a lighter tethering than the spell that had saved RJ's life, and reversible although RJ had no plans to let that happen.

"You had to take responsibility for me when they let me into the Bureau," RJ had argued. *"This is me making it very clear that I'm not going anywhere without you. Like a bail bond, only better."*

The hot sun didn't agree with RJ's ginger coloring, so he spent most of his time underneath an umbrella while Bart lounged next to him in the sun, turning a delicious shade of toasted marshmallow. RJ had plans to map all those tan lines with his tongue when they took a shower.

Key West turned out to be everything RJ hoped, with plenty of nightlife, amazing Cuban and Caribbean food, and a nightly celebration on the beach to watch the sunset. He already knew he wanted to come back with Bart again and again.

By the time they headed to their room, RJ was relaxed—and horny. He pushed Bart against the door as soon as they were inside, slotting himself between his legs and rubbing his erection against Bart's rapidly thickening cock.

"How about we do round one in the shower so we don't make a total mess of the sheets?" Bart murmured.

RJ was ready to sluice off the sweat and sunscreen, though he had a mess of a different sort in mind once they got to bed.

The walk-in shower was big enough for both of them, and RJ didn't waste time once they stripped down and rinsed off. He dropped to his knees in front of Bart and took a moment to ogle his lover's endowments before swallowing him down.

"Easy, tiger," Bart jokingly chided. "We aren't teenagers. Round two might end up waiting until after dinner."

RJ pulled off and shot Bart a smutty grin. "You know what they say...fuck around and find out." He returned to his work in earnest, licking and sucking until Bart shot his load down RJ's throat. He licked the last few drops of jizz from his lips with a satisfied smile.

"You're really good at that." Bart sounded breathless.

"We've been practicing a lot." RJ rose to his feet and kissed Bart, letting him taste himself.

"Turn around," Bart murmured against his ear. RJ complied, settling his back against Bart's chest, giving him perfect access to return the favor. RJ let his head fall back against Bart's shoulder as Bart wrapped his hand around RJ's cock, setting up a slow rhythm that drove RJ crazy. RJ wriggled back against Bart's still-soft-but-definitely-interested dick that nestled in the cleft of his ass, a promise of things to come.

"More," RJ panted. A day by the pool filled with hot bodies in skimpy wet suits had given him plenty of ideas for what he wanted from his lover once they were behind closed doors.

Bart quickened his strokes, and RJ rewarded him with a moan that left nothing to the imagination. RJ might have been embarrassed by how quickly he shot off if it weren't for having just delivered an extremely sexy blow job that left him hard and aching.

They washed and shampooed, not wanting to be late for dinner. Bart had found a lovely beachfront resort that catered to gay couples, with a dining room and chef that fed them into a food coma each night.

RJ thought Bart looked particularly handsome in the pale blue linen camp shirt over long tan shorts and flip-flops. Several knotted leather bracelets replaced his usual watch, a clear nod to being on "island time." They had splurged on some new clothes before the vacation, dropping a bundle at Tommy Bahama, but RJ was convinced it was worth every penny.

"You look good enough to eat," he told Bart with a lascivious grin.

"I was just thinking the same thing about you." Bart gave RJ an appreciative look that made him want to preen. RJ had to admit that the low-key island print shirt worked well with his coloring and coordinated with his light sand-colored drawstring capris and leather flip-flops. Bracelets with shells and sea glass gave the outfit a "beachy" feel.

"I'm glad you like what you see. I'll be glad to give you a private showing after dinner," RJ growled.

They had a perfect meal in the restaurant's intimate dining room with a view of the ocean. RJ sent his compliments to the chef for his scallops over risotto with a pineapple and mango salad. Bart was equally pleased by his order of shrimp and grits with a side of conch fritters. Not wanting to be wiped out by a heavy dinner after a day in the sun, they both ordered Aperol Spritzes, knowing a bottle of prosecco awaited them in their room for later.

Afterward, as they stood on the beach surrounded by locals and tourists for the nightly sunset celebration, RJ reached out to take Bart's hand.

"This is perfect." RJ knew that Bart could read his feelings in his eyes as well as in their bond. "Have I mentioned how much I love you?"

Bart sidled closer so that they were in contact from shoulders to hips. "I definitely feel the love." The emotion was clear in his voice.

RJ watched the sunset paint the sky and the ocean in shades of pink, orange, and indigo. "Oh, yeah. And I'm planning on feeling more of it when we're back in the room."

Despite their pornographic promises, Bart and RJ took their time strolling along the beach. The stars glowed more brightly here, and the moon sent a silver pathway along the waves. They stopped for Key Lime gelato and savored the treat as they retraced their steps to the resort.

Bart opened the prosecco when they returned to the room and handed a flute of the bubbly drink to RJ. "To us."

RJ didn't need alcohol to make him feel mellow, and he had shed his inhibitions with Bart long ago. When he finished his drink, he set the crystal glass aside and began a slow striptease, first his open island shirt, then the tee beneath it, complete with sexy gyrations and an unmistakable bump-and-grind as he swiveled his hips to shed his capris.

"You're killing me." Bart palmed his hard cock to avoid going off too soon. "God, you could charge money for that. I'd slip some bills in your G-string any day."

RJ grinned. "I had a job as a dancer at a club when I was in my early twenties, between festival gigs. Strictly look but don't touch. The tips were great." He sidled up to Bart wearing nothing but a smile. "But you can touch me anywhere you want, big boy."

Bart had made record time getting out of his clothes. RJ gave a surprised yelp as Bart cupped his ass and picked him up, pushing his back against the wall.

"This okay?" Bart asked, although from the way RJ locked his ankles behind Bart's back and his tattle-tale boner, RJ didn't need words to reply. Good thing because he was too busy nipping and kissing his way down Bart's neck.

"Don't leave marks they'll see at the office," Bart rumbled, updating his rules from their first encounter.

"Nobody but me will see," RJ promised, sucking a hickey into the skin over Bart's heart.

RJ had finished their shower exploits by letting Bart open him before they went to dinner. Now Bart opened a packet of lube he had palmed from his pocket to slick up his cock and slid two fingers into RJ's channel, followed by a third.

"Still ready for me?" he murmured, licking at the shell of RJ's ear and making him tremble.

"What 'cha waiting for? Fuck me already," RJ panted, impatient.

He gasped and arched in Bart's arms as his lover pulled his ass cheeks apart and sank balls-deep. He couldn't move much backed up against the wall, but RJ managed to swivel his hips in a figure-eight, goading Bart to pick up the pace.

Bart set up a slow rocking rhythm, making sure to hit RJ's sweet spot just right. RJ nipped and tugged at Bart's nipples and licked a stripe up his neck. His hard-as-steel cock was trapped between their bellies, getting plenty of friction. Just as RJ felt himself tip over the edge, he sensed a surge of emotion through the invisible bond.

Love. Desire. Affection. Forever.

That was enough to make him climax, spilling his come between them. Bart only lasted for a few more thrusts before he filled RJ's ass with his warm seed. They stayed where they were for several moments afterward, panting and sweaty, breathing in each other's air. RJ's legs wrapped around Bart's waist, and Bart's magic tangled around their souls.

"Not bad," RJ drawled with a broad grin. "We've done the shower and the wall. How about we break in the bed next? Best two out of three?"

AFTERWORD

I'm so thrilled to be part of the multi-author, shared-world Carnival of Mysteries series! Please make sure you check out all the books and our Facebook reader group.

Bart and RJ also show up in my Kings of the Mountain series, several years after this book, when they have settled into their work roles and their ongoing relationship. You can find more of their exploits there.

ACKNOWLEDGMENTS

Thank you so much to my editor, Jean Rabe, to my husband and writing partner, Larry N. Martin for all his behind-the-scenes hard work, to my beta readers, and to my wonderful cover artist Dianne Thies. Thanks also to the Shadow Alliance and the Worlds of Morgan Brice reader street teams for their support and encouragement, plus my promotional crew and the ever-growing legion of ARC readers who help spread the word!

I couldn't do it without you! And, of course, thanks and love to my "convention gang" of fellow authors for making road trips and virtual cons fun.

ABOUT THE AUTHOR

Morgan Brice is the romance pen name of bestselling author Gail Z. Martin. Morgan writes urban fantasy male/male paranormal romance, with plenty of action, adventure, and supernatural thrills to go with the happily ever after.

Gail writes epic fantasy and urban fantasy, and together with co-author hubby Larry N. Martin, steampunk and comedic horror, all of which have less romance and more explosions.

On the rare occasions Morgan isn't writing, she's either reading, cooking, or spoiling two very pampered dogs.

Watch for additional new series from Morgan Brice and more books in the Witchbane, Badlands, Treasure Trail, Kings of the Mountain, Sharps & Springfield, and Fox Hollow universes coming soon!

Where to find me, and how to stay in touch

Join my Worlds of Morgan Brice Facebook Group and get in on all the behind-the-scenes fun! My free reader group is the first to see cover reveals, learn tidbits about works-in-progress, have fun with exclusive contests and giveaways, find out about in-person get-togethers, and more! It's also where I find my beta readers, ARC readers, and launch team! Come join the party!
https://www.Facebook.com/groups/WorldsOfMorganBrice
Find me on the web at https://morganbrice.com. Sign up for my newsletter and never miss a new release! http://eepurl.-

com/dy_8oL. You can also find me on X (formerly Twitter): @MorganBriceBook, on Pinterest (for Morgan and Gail): pinterest.com/Gzmartin, on Instagram as MorganBriceAuthor, on YouTube at https://www.youtube.com/c/GailZ-MartinAuthor/ on Bookbub https://www.bookbub.com/authors/morgan-brice and now on TikTok @MorganBriceAuthor

Check out the ongoing, online convention ConTinual www.facebook.com/groups/ConTinual

Support Indie Authors

When you support independent authors, you help influence what kind of books you'll see and what types of stories will be available because the authors themselves decide what to write, not a big publishing conglomerate. Independent authors are local creators supporting their families with the books they produce. Thank you for supporting independent authors and small press fiction!

MORE BY MORGAN BRICE

Badlands Series

Badlands

Restless Nights, a Badlands Short Story

Lucky Town, a Badlands Novella

The Rising

Cover Me, a Badlands Short Story

Loose Ends

Leap of Faith, a Badlands/Witchbane Novella

Night, a Badlands Short Story

No Surrender

Warm You Up, a Badlands Short Story

Point Blank

Fox Hollow Zodiac Series

Huntsman

Again

Fox Hollow Universe

Romp, a Fox Hollow Novella

Nutty for You, a Fox Hollow Short Story

Imaginary Lover

Haven

Gruff

Trash and Treasure

CARNIVAL OF MYSTERIES

Welcome, Traveler! Join us for a series of M/M fantasies by a talented group of both new and established authors. Whether you enjoy mystery, action, danger, or just sweet romance, there is something for everyone at the Carnival of Mysteries!

Kim Fielding * L. A. Witt * Kaje Harper

Megan Derr * Ander C. Lark * E. J. Russell

Morgan Brice * Sarah Ellis * Kayleigh Sky

Nicole Dennis * Elizabeth Silver * Ro Merrill

T. A. Moore * Z. A. Maxfield

Rachel Langella